FIRST CONTACT...

Shelby suddenly heard a roaring sound and, almost immediately afterward, the sharp report of an exploding seed pod. She drew her weapon and pushed through into a small clearing. She fired at the long, sinewy form. It fell to the ground, dead. It was a hellhound, and it had severely mauled a Shade.

Shelby stared at the poor being, stunned. The Shade had literally been ripped open. It was still alive but dying fast. And there was absolutely nothing she could do. It looked at her and there was no expression of pain upon its face, but there was agony in those bright violet eyes that seemed to shimmer. Slowly, the Shade reached out with one hand and touched her. *She felt a searing blast of pain, like a fireball exploding in her mind . . .*

Last Communion

by
Nicholas Yermakov

A SIGNET BOOK
NEW AMERICAN LIBRARY
TIMES MIRROR

NAL BOOKS ARE AVAILABLE AT QUANTITY DISCOUNTS WHEN USED TO PROMOTE PRODUCTS OR SERVICES. FOR INFORMATION PLEASE WRITE TO PREMIUM MARKETING DIVISION, THE NEW AMERICAN LIBRARY, INC., 1633 BROADWAY, NEW YORK, NEW YORK 10019.

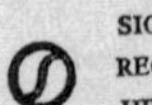

SIGNET TRADEMARK REG. U.S. PAT. OFF. AND FOREIGN COUNTRIES
REGISTERED TRADEMARK—MARCA REGISTRADA
HECHO EN CHICAGO, U.S.A.

SIGNET, SIGNET CLASSICS, MENTOR, PLUME, MERIDIAN AND NAL BOOKS *are published by The New American Library, Inc., 1633 Broadway, New York, New York 10019*

FIRST PRINTING, JUNE, 1981

1 2 3 4 5 6 7 8 9

PRINTED IN THE UNITED STATES OF AMERICA

PUBLISHER'S NOTE

For Ed Bryant,

with special thanks to the survivors of Milford '80—(clockwise, around the table) Bill Wu, Karl Hansen, George Guthridge, Pamela Lifton-Zoline, Cynthia Felice, Kevin O'Donnell, Jr. (skip . . . a space for yours truly), Connie Willis, Pat Hodgell, Carol Emshwiller, Mike Toman, and last, but by no means the least, George R. R. Martin, who, if I hadn't carried him down that Colorado mountain trail, would never have been able to collect his two Hugos.

PROLOGUE

Wendy Chan lay sprawled upon the forest floor, tears making tracks in the dirt that caked her face, fingers clutching at the earth. She whimpered like a child and lowered her head onto a section of gnarled root at the base of a large tree that draped its large fronds over her. She had been running aimlessly through the forest, oblivious of the branches that lashed her face, lacerating her about the cheeks and eyes. She was bruised and battered from her flight and drenched with sweat. She was physically exhausted, but she felt no pain. No physical pain. It seemed to her that she was isolated, lost inside her head, divorced not only from her body, but from all of her surroundings too.

Hours before, there had been some vague homing instinct that had driven her toward the ship's lighter, toward the closest thing to home that existed for her on an alien world. But that homing instinct was long gone. It had been driven out by panic and hysteria until all that remained was an animal urge to flee, to somehow find someone or something to which she could hold onto, something familiar, some reassurance that the fragile fabric of her reality had not been torn to shreds. There was a maelstrom in her mind that would not subside. She tried with all her will to fight it, but she broke.

The defeated creature that huddled on the ground bore slight resemblance to Lieutenant Win T'ao Chan, a resilient and highly trained specialist, an officer in Colonization Command. The last thing that Lieutenant Chan had seen had been a pair of shockingly violet eyes that seemed to burn with an opalescent fire. That image still lingered, but Lieutenant Chan was gone.

The rays of light that threaded through the treetops dimmed. Night fell and the crescent-shaped moon of Boomerang tumbled lazily across the sky in its low, fast orbit. The forest took on a new and even more foreboding aspect as the predators began their nightly concert. Wendy didn't hear them.

She was quiet now, motionless upon the ground. The tears still flowed, but she couldn't feel them. They ran into the corners of her mouth and she was unaware of their salty taste. She shivered even though the night was warm.

A fist-sized beetle detached itself from the tree and crawled onto her head. It nestled momentarily in her hair, twitching its mandibles. It tugged briefly at a lock of straight black hair, then continued on its way across her neck and shoulders and down onto the ground, where it fell, landing on its back. Its legs fumbled at the air.

The pulse sent out by the communicator strapped to Wendy's wrist was what led them to her. They found her lying there, looking very dead.

"Oh, Jesus," Fannon said, rushing to her side. He kneeled down and felt for a pulse. "She's alive." He sighed.

Nils Björnsen crouched down and helped Fannon turn her over. He cradled her head in his lap.

"Wendy. Wendy? Can you hear me?"

There was no response. Her eyes were open, but they weren't seeing anything. At least they weren't seeing what was before them.

"What's wrong with her?" asked Fannon. "Christ, what happened?"

"I don't know." Björnsen glanced about him nervously. "I'm not going to try to find out here."

There was a rustling in the underbrush not far away.

"Let's get her back to the ship as fast as possible."

The breath whooshed out of her softly as Drew Fannon lifted her up onto his shoulders, a dead weight like a sack of flour. Nils Björnsen unslung his rifle and followed his companion back to the lighter. Some time later, the lighter took off, heading toward a rendezvous with the larger ship in orbit around Boomerang. It left behind a burned-out clearing and a night that was anything but still.

CHAPTER ONE

She looked so peaceful lying there, like a naked water sprite preserved in ice. As the mist slowly cleared, Drew Fannon looked away. Although he had been in coldsleep many times himself, he always felt uneasy seeing someone else inside a cryogen. Something about coldsleep made people look like corpses embedded in sapphire quartz. It was a grim reminder of the many times that he himself had dreamed in limbo. Cryogen dreams were long and very vivid, and Fannon was prone to nightmares.

"She'll be awake soon," he said.

Nils Björnsen approached the cryogen and looked inside. He didn't share his crewmate's problem, but he looked nervous just the same.

"I really wish we didn't have to do this," Nils said.

"Have we got a choice?" asked Fannon.

"No."

Nils stared long and hard at the form inside the chamber. He sighed and shook his head.

"Hell, she's a *pilot*."

"So? Did they tell you it was going to be easy?"

"She also outranks us both. She could just order us to put her back to sleep again."

"In that case, the colonel's going to have a small mutiny on her hands," said Fannon.

"She can bring us up on charges when we get back."

"Let's worry about getting back, first. Besides, when

ColCom learns that it was a choice between reviving the pilot or scrubbing the mission, they'll see it our way."

Björnsen continued to stare down into the cryogen, and Fannon scowled. A chime began to sound.

"Well, it's a little late for second thoughts now."

The clear dome top of the cryogen slid back like a retracting coffin lid. The nude body of Colonel Shelby Michaels lay exposed. Her chest rose and fell rhythmically, and after a few moments her eyelids flickered open. Neither man spoke as they both waited for her to come fully awake. They had stepped back and they now watched in silence as she flexed and relaxed her muscles, clenched and unclenched her fists, trying to banish the stiffness that always accompanied revival from coldsleep. There would be some dizziness and perhaps some nausea, as well as a brief period of disorientation.

She might not be able to speak at first, thought Fannon. He always came out of coldsleep with a sore throat and an unresponsive larynx. Maybe she wouldn't be able to; he almost hoped so.

She sat up slowly and dangled a leg off the side of the cryogen. Then, assisting herself awkwardly with her arms, she swiveled around. And saw them. She stared blankly, then became clearly frightened. Her mouth opened, but no sound came forth. She jerked involuntarily and lost her balance, falling to the deck with a splatting sound. Neither Nils nor Fannon had been able to move quickly enough to catch her.

"Hell," said Nils, as he struggled with her weight. He couldn't quite manage to lift her. She was not a small woman.

"Is she all right?" asked Fannon.

"I think so. Looks like she just fainted. Help me with her."

"Swell. We're off to a great start."

Nils glared at him but said nothing. Fannon helped him lift Shelby onto one of the flight chairs. There was a thin trickle of blood coming from one of her nostrils.

"Drew, get the medpak out of sick bay, will you?"

Fannon left, being careful not to look at the one cryogen still occupied as he went past it. Sleep well, Wendy, he thought. God, you never should have come. Maybe they'll be able to cure you when we get back. That's if they ever figure out what's wrong with you.

It looked almost like a dance.

The Shades circled each other cautiously, alertly, looking for an opening, a sign of weakness, a momentary lapse in concentration. There was an eerie, ritualistic quality about it that was mesmerizing. Both creatures were tall, much taller than an average human, and very finely boned. They were beautiful to look at. Their muscles rippled beneath their steel-gray skin and their reproductive organs were retracted. Long albino hair cascaded down over their shoulders like manes. They leaped forward as one.

"How about that?" Fannon said, his voice coming from just behind Shelby. "It's some sort of challenge ritual. They look like a couple of stags going at it."

Shelby shut her eyes briefly, wincing. She had been so involved in watching the screen that she had almost forgotten about the presence of the two men. Now she was painfully aware of their proximity. She tried to turn her attention back to the screen.

As the Shades attacked each other, their weapons lay forgotten on the ground where they had dropped them: long, slender hunting javelins, sturdy stone axes, the curiously curved nutfruit slings. They fought with open hands, either slapping hard or striking with the heels of their palms. They came together, exchanged a flurry of blows and sprang apart to start circling once again. It almost seemed choreographed, like a ballet.

"Notice that they had recourse to their weapons, but they're not using them," Fannon whispered to her as she watched the screen. She focused all her attention on the spectacle before her, trying to forget the two men sitting just behind her, trying to will them out of existence.

The confrontation was repeated, and the Shades separated once again. Neither seemed to be breathing hard. The third time, they locked together like two wrestlers. Their inhuman flexibility was evident as they strained against each other, each trying to force the other into an inferior position. This new contest didn't last very long. With a sudden effort, one of the Shades forced the other to its knees. The beaten Shade immediately stopped struggling. The victor stepped back while the other remained kneeling, head bowed.

Here it comes, thought Shelby, as the standing Shade grasped its opponent by its mane of white hair and pulled its face up, exposing the throat. But instead of striking a lethal blow, the victorious Shade merely placed the heel of its hand against the forehead of the other, held it there briefly, then stepped away. The defeated Shade then stood up, collected its weapons and slowly walked away into the forest. The remaining Shade also gathered up its weapons, then turned and stared directly at the camera.

"We were lying in concealment," said Nils. "We thought it couldn't see us. Either we were wrong or it smelled us or one of us made a sound and somehow attracted its attention."

The picture lurched suddenly.

"This is where I stood up," said Fannon. "I got up in full view of it, to see what it would do."

It ignored them. The Shade calmly turned away from the camera and disappeared into the trees. The screen continued to show an empty clearing for a moment, then it went blank.

"It's a classic animal-dominance, territorial-imperative pattern," said Nils. Shelby did not turn around, continuing to stare at the blank screen. "It bears out my theory about their individual domain structure."

He paused and glanced at Fannon. Drew was looking at Shelby's hunched shoulders, his lips drawn tight. It wasn't working. They had thought that discussing their findings might make it easier for her to grow accustomed to them, shoptalk instead of more intimate and, to her, more threatening conversation. But she had yet to say a word. The aftereffects of coldsleep should have worn off by now, thought Nils. Or was it the coldsleep? Shelby Michaels was scared stiff. Nils had no idea what to do about that. He had never spoken to a pilot before. But then neither had anyone else.

"We've established that they clash over domain," Nils continued, not knowing what else to do, "but if this was a typical example, then it would seem that these conflicts are not generally fatal. Perhaps they could be, either through accident or if one Shade refused to yield to the other, but it appears that the entire point is to establish only which of them is the stronger. Then the weaker one simply backs off."

Was he talking to himself? She showed no sign of hearing him. She kept staring intently at the empty screen.

Nils hesitated, glanced at Fannon once again, saw his shrug and continued. "The significant aspect here is that both of them could have used their weapons, but they didn't. Was it frenzy, or *choice*? We came upon them as they were circling each other. We never saw the start. That's a damn shame. I find the Shades absolutely fascinating. Animal-dominance behavior coupled with toolmaking capabilities and an almost human . . . hell, more than human restraint. That Shade could have killed the other one. It didn't, though. An animal would have, I think. I can't make up my mind. Are they sentient humanoids or highly advanced animals?"

"Perhaps they're sentient animals," said Fannon dryly.

"Did they make any sounds?" asked Shelby.

There was a sudden silence as both men started, then stared at each other. Her first words since reviving from coldsleep. Nils exhaled heavily, with relief. Maybe it'll be all right, he thought. Please . . .

"You mean like cries or snarls?" said Fannon, anxious to get her talking. "No, there was nothing like that. It was all eerily silent. Interesting that you should pick up on that, Colonel. You think maybe they don't have any vocal chords?"

She didn't respond.

"Well, that wouldn't necessarily preclude their ability to make some sort of sounds," said Nils, aghast at Fannon's insensitivity. "They do seem to be mute, though. Sort of like Terran giraffes. If they are sentient, that would explain their noncommunicativeness. We obviously don't fit into their experience, so they might perceive that we're no threat to them and simply accept our presence, much as a fish might accept the presence of an underwater cable, for example. We've just become part of their background. Still, that doesn't seem like sentient behavior, does it? It's a puzzle. A puzzle we're going to have to solve before we submit our colonization report on Boomerang."

"Listen, Colonel . . ." Fannon leaned forward and touched her shoulder. Her entire body jerked as if there had been current flowing through his fingers. In one electric spasm, she leaped from the chair, knocked into the screen and bolted, running from the room. The hatch hissed shut behind her.

"Goddammit, Drew! You had to go and touch her, didn't you?"

Fannon scowled. "Well, I didn't think she'd—"

"That's just it, you didn't think!"

Drew Fannon flushed and rose to his feet angrily. "Look, lay off, okay? It's tough enough, what with what happened to Wendy. On top of that, now we've got to nursemaid a pilot. I always thought they were a weird bunch. She gives me the creeps."

"Well, you're just going to have to get over that in one great big hurry," Nils said. "We *need* her, Drew. And she's the one who's got to get us back when we enter cold-sleep at the end of this. Or have you forgotten? Upsetting our pilot is the last thing we need to do."

"Okay, you're right, I didn't mean it. I didn't think. You're right, as usual. I don't know what's gotten into me. It's just that Wendy—"

"I know, Drew. I'm not exactly made of stone myself."

"Yeah. Shit. I'm sorry. What are we going to do about her?"

"I don't know. Try to make her feel safe with us, somehow." Nils rubbed the bridge of his nose. "I don't think there's ever been a precedent for this. The regulations regarding fraternization with pilots are quite specific."

"The people who make the regulations don't have to live with them out in the field," replied Fannon.

"I can almost understand how she must feel," said Björnsen. "I feel the same way every time I come back from a mission. Everything changed; I don't belong, somehow. We're not exactly normal ourselves, you know."

Fannon leaned against the bulkhead wearily. "Tell me about it. But I hardly think it's the same thing. I don't jump out of my boots at the mere sight of another human face."

"You know," said Nils, "I've always wondered what it must be like for a pilot. Living out their lives in space, never leaving the ship, always alone with nothing but a ship's computer for company. It must be hell. How do they stand it?"

"Well, now's your chance to find out." Fannon started toward the cryogen where Wendy slept, but stopped half-way across the room. He couldn't bring himself to look at her lying there, beyond his reach.

"Why did she have to go out alone?" he said.

Nils had no answer.

"She never should have come. She's too fragile for this type of work. She should have stayed back at ColCom HQ, where she belongs."

"And Shelby should have stayed in coldsleep, where she belongs," said Nils. "But we needed her with us, for better or for worse. And ColCom needed Wendy out here. What's that line from the old poem, 'Ours not to reason why'?"

"Spare me, willya?"

"Lighten up, Drew. Don't go getting tense on me."

Fannon sat down and drummed his fingers on the arm of the flight chair. Then he made a fist and slammed it down hard. "What *happened* out there?"

"Your guess is as good as mine," said Nils. "Maybe nothing. Maybe you're right. Perhaps she was too fragile for this kind of work. Maybe she just couldn't take it and she broke."

"Could be. But then you and I aren't exactly one hundred percent ourselves. Look at us, we're on edge, we're snapping at each other. People like us just don't get frayed nerves. Something's getting to us, Nils." He paused, deep in thought. "What if there's some sort of virus . . ."

"There's no trace of anything foreign in Wendy's system. At least, nothing I can identify," said Nils. "If I was a psychiatrist, I'd be able to make a more educated guess, perhaps. *Something* happened. What, I don't know. She's catatonic. Whatever it was she was experiencing, it seems she couldn't handle it, so she's withdrawn."

"That's a pretty specific guess for someone who's not a shrink."

"It's the best one I can make, under the circumstances. I could be way off, but there's nothing physically wrong with her, except some superficial wounds and lacerations. How do *you* feel, by the way?"

"You mean physically?"

"I know how you feel physically."

"Oh." Fannon rubbed his eyes and winced. "Okay, truth time?"

Björnsen nodded.

"I don't like this place. Don't ask me why, I can't put my finger on it. I've been on worse missions, Lord knows. This world is beautiful, it's everything I like. It's clean, it's unspoiled, it's . . . I don't know. I should be completely in my element here . . . and yet . . ." He hesitated. "I feel a little homesick."

"Homesick?"

"Yeah. Isn't that ridiculous? We don't *have* a home."

She sat curled up in her cabin, staring intently at the screen in front of her. All the information gathered by the survey team to date, all the work done by Wendy, Nils and Fannon, was in the computer program she was running. She devoured the information, fastening onto the data as a drowning person might clutch at straws. There was no way out. She had the authority to order them to place her back in coldsleep, but she couldn't exercise it. It was an emergency situation. One of the team had fallen ill somehow, and they needed her. She felt responsible for them. It had been her job to get the team to Boomerang safely. Technically, her responsibility ended there. Get them there and get them back. The mission itself was none of her concern, but she couldn't let it go at that.

Countless times, during the journey, while she was in and out of coldsleep, monitoring ship's functions, checking on their life-support systems while they were in the cryogens, she had seen their faces through the sapphire mist. They were familiar faces, and yet they were strangers. She didn't know them. She didn't want to know them, but she couldn't shake her feelings of responsibility toward them. They were her charges. She was the ranking officer. None of that should have made any difference, according to the regulations. But still . . .

She ran the program again, feeling itchy from the cold sweat running down her back. She tried to will herself to relax, but all her muscles seemed to have bunched into knots.

Boomerang was in the system of a type G yellow dwarf. The diameter of the planet was 15,120.724 km. The letters "furex avcom" appeared on the screen—"further extrapolation available from the computer." She let it go. There was one continental landmass, approximately 138,000 square km, formed by a collision of two smaller continental masses approximately fifteen million years ago. The collision formed a massive mountain range down the center of the new continent, rising to heights of 50 to 60,000 meters. The gravity was .75 (3/4 Earth specific), because of a lower core density. That accounted, in part, for the Shades being taller and more fine-boned than humans. The survey team reported feeling lighter and springier in the thinner atmosphere, which was breathable, but took some getting used to. They were all more muscular than the Shades, she realized, but the Shades had longer bones, so there wouldn't be much of a strength advantage, and they seemed to have quicker reflexes, judging from the tapes she had seen.

Why did that seem important? Paranoid reasoning? According to all available data, the Shades did not appear to be a threat, but then she felt threatened by her own survey team. She leaned back against the bulkhead, shutting her eyes. She couldn't bear to be in the same room with the two men. They seemed as alien to her as did the Shades. Fannon had named them that; they seemed like ghostly beings, wraiths. Fannon. He made her insides churn. Years and years ago, there had been someone very much like Fannon . . . She pushed the thought out of her mind with an effort.

The mountains were surrounded by very heavily forested regions. The planet had a less severe axial tilt than Earth, which gave it more temperate weather overall, although the equatorial regions were very hot. The polar icecaps were smaller and the seasons were of a more uniform length than Earth's. There was no snow. Precipitation was divided fairly evenly among the seasons. There was desert at the equatorial belt.

She was only picking up on isolated snatches of the programming. She couldn't concentrate. It galled her. The ship's computer was her only friend. She used its library to pass the time during the journey, she played chess with it and backgammon and countless other games, but now it provided but a slight distraction. She had to familiarize herself with the data accumulated by the team, but the members of the team itself were foremost in her mind.

She stuffed her knuckles into her mouth and bit down on them. I've got to learn how to function with them somehow, she thought. What am I going to do?

The lesser gravity of Boomerang resulted in very tall and fairly slender trees. The animals indigenous to the world would tend to be built more along the lines of antelope and puma than buffalo and grizzly bears. They could be big, but not as massive as elephants. There was a greater variety of flying creatures. . . .

It was too much. She couldn't sort it out. She missed half of what flashed by on the screen. She kept having to stop and go back over the data. Chan had entered most of the data, and since her specialty was zoology she kept making comparisons to Terran life forms. It brought back too many unpleasant memories. She had joined the service to get away from Earth. As far away as possible. Away from everything she knew. Away from other people. . . .

The information now on the screen concerned the Shades, the beings who had become the central aspect of the mission. They seemed to have a primitive, supra-agrarian culture, fulfilling the role of primary link in the world's ecological chain. For all the ferocity of the other animals on Boomerang, the Shades appeared to be the main predators. They had an extremely strong sense of territorial imperative, as Nils had pointed out. She tried not to think about Nils. Each native had a "domain" that it hunted and cared for, and there was now evidence that they sometimes clashed over domain. However, unlike animals, the Shades seemed to possess a degree of sentience, and they were more intricately involved in maintaining their domains than any ordinary predator would be, at least by Terran standards. In addition to hunting or foraging off the flora, each Shade would care for the sick plants and animals in its domain, often in fairly complex ways. The team had observed Shades using intricate knowledge of mosses and lichens to aid diseased plants. They had seen streams rerouted. This was all evidence of very advanced sentience, and yet the natives did not live in groups. There was no discernible tribal structure, and there was no evidence of any communication among the natives. How then did each native acquire the wide range of knowledge necessary to enable it to survive in such a harsh environment?

Several Shades had been seen with young, but never more than one. How did they reproduce? And were the young born only one at a time? How were they raised without a family unit in a seemingly sentient non-society? Even animals had family units, after a fashion. How did they communicate with one another? Or didn't they? But that was impossible.

Little by little, Shelby felt herself drawn into the puzzle of the Shades and forgetting her anxiety at being suddenly thrown together with Björnsen and Fannon. This was something she could handle, something she could relate to. It was a problem. And every problem had a solution. The thing was finding it. Given enough information, any problem could be solved. Shelby found herself becoming hooked.

The Shades made tools, but they didn't construct shelters. At least the team had found no evidence of any. They possessed a limited degree of sophistication, yet they lived apart. They seemed to share certain types of knowledge, but there was no evidence of any sort of communication among Shades, and they showed not the slightest bit of interest in the humans observing them. And they kept their distance.

For some strange reason, Shelby found herself thinking about a pet her parents had given her when she was a child. It had been a beautiful gray Persian cat, rather the same color as the Shades. Only the animal had been full-grown, not affectionate as a kitten would have been. It had wanted nothing to do with Shelby. It resisted all her attempts to pet it. Every time she got near it, the cat would walk away. If she entered the room the cat was in, it would merely look up at her in a bored fashion, establish her presence, then ignore her once again. The most Shelby had been able to accomplish was a state of peaceful coexistence with the animal. It had never become her friend. It had never shown her the least bit of affection. All her efforts directed toward making the cat love her had been in vain, and she had been crushed.

Her parents had never had much time for her. Perhaps that was why they had given her the cat, but that resulted only in further heartbreak. Then her parents had died when she was still very young. Gone away and left her. And that had set the pattern for the remainder of her life. Shelby felt tears coming from her eyes. By Terran standard time, all that had happened long, long ago. She hadn't thought about those things for many, many years. Why now? Why all of a sudden?

Perhaps, in a way, she was now the cat. Fannon seemed to be a hard man, but he had tried to get through to her, in his own rough way. And Nils Björnsen had tried to be kind. They hadn't come after her when she had fled the room. The door to the cabin was closed, but they hadn't tried to gain admission. Hours had gone by while she remained closeted in her cabin. What were they doing? What must they think of her?

A freak, that's what they must think, she said to herself. They think they're stuck with a freak. She had often wondered how spacers must feel about their pilots, whom they never see except inside a cryogen. To trust their safety to a total stranger must be very hard. And yet she had to do no less. When her phase of the mission was over and she entered coldsleep for the duration of a team's assignment, she was the one who had to depend on them while she dreamed. It wasn't always that way, she knew. In the old days, there had been no stark division between pilot and crew. But then the time factor involved and the cost effectiveness of frequent periods in and out of coldsleep had caused ColCom to realize that truly long voyages would be impractical. The stresses that were placed upon crewmembers as they were awakened for periods of time throughout the journeys resulted in friction and psychological disorientation. It was far more practical to recruit a certain type of individual, the sort of person who, on Earth, would be a recluse or a patient in some sanitarium. The sort of person who, for a multitude of reasons, not only could handle being alone, but could not function any other way. "Self-contained" was the term that was used a lot. No one ever said the word "insane." At least, not out loud.

The service had saved her life. It *was* her life. She could not imagine herself doing anything else. She had no need of material possessions, no desire for the company of her fellow human beings. The lack of any sort of sexual activity meant nothing to her. She was not a virgin. There had been a man, once. But it was best not to think about that. As a pilot, she could involve herself in the one thing that meant anything to her, the pursuit of knowledge. The computers were her teachers and her friends. The irony that she was probably better educated than the other members of her team was not lost on her. But ivory-tower academics are one thing, putting that knowledge to work is another, she thought. From a purely theoretical standpoint, she was well aware of what her problems were. She was fully aware of the nature of her insecurities and the factors that motivated them, but knowing what a problem was and dealing with it were two separate things.

She knew a great deal about Nils Björnsen and Drew Fannon. She had access to their dossiers, their classified ColCom files. As a pilot, she had that privilege, whereas the other members of the crew did not. Yet she had never exercised it before. Somehow it was always better for her to deal with her charges in a purely mechanical manner. The less she knew of them the better. But now, things were different. Like it or not, she would have to work with the two men. She didn't like it, but she had no choice. Not if the mission was to succeed. I won't let them intimidate me, she thought. I won't!

"I say we try to force some contact somehow," Fannon said.

"I'm not so sure that would be a good idea at this point," said Nils. "I'd be much more at ease with continuing passive observation until we have something more to work with. We still have a lot to learn. Let's not push it."

"Look, they've got to have *some* form of communication," Fannon continued, "even if it's only of the 'do-as-I-do' animal variety. If we can figure out a way to break through to them, even if it's only on that level, hell, it's still something that will allow us to function with them!"

"That's true," said Nils, "but I wouldn't want to try to *force* the contact. They don't presently regard us as a threat. Let's not give them any grounds to change their minds. I've got an idea, though it goes against all standard procedure and it might prove dangerous."

"Let's hear it," Shelby said, feeling a lump in her throat. It had been all she could do to get the words out. They had managed to reach a level of coexistence that was shaky at best. Both men deferred to her rank, even to the point of addressing her as "Colonel," rather than calling her by name, which presupposed a relationship of greater intimacy. It was a small enough thing, but it helped to give her a sense of distance from them. And they were very careful not only not to touch her or accidentally brush against her in any way, but to avoid looking directly at her.

They're trying, Shelby thought. They're really trying. So why is it so goddam *hard*?

Nils briefly glanced in her direction and then looked at Fannon. He leaned forward in the flight chair of the lighter and bit his lower lip. Outside, it was getting on toward evening on Boomerang.

"Okay. Are you familiar with the ancient fable of Androcles and the lion? In the story, a man called Androcles comes upon a lion with a thorn in its paw. He summons up the courage to remove it, and the animal, recognizing the kind act, becomes his friend. Suppose we did something nice for our friends the Shades? Something they could understand and take good advantage of? They're foragers and sophisticated hunters, right? Suppose we introduced them to the concept of archery?"

There was a long silence. Fannon let his breath out slowly.

"Oh, boy. And you said it *might* prove dangerous?"

"Not much more dangerous than those seed-pod catapults they use," replied Shelby. She looked pointedly at the floor and found that the words came easier that way.

"How so, Colonel?" asked Fannon, softly.

She hesitated, still not looking at him. "Well, from what I gather, those seed-pod hurlers are potentially more lethal than arrows. An arrow might only wound, whereas you've reported that inhaling the powder from an exploded seed pod is certain death. And they haven't used those against you, have they? Even though they've had several opportunities. Am I correct?"

"You are."

"Bows and arrows, even fairly primitive ones, could increase their range over the catapults. I'd be interested to see how they would react. It would be possible for them to grasp the concept of archery and to take it one step further by, say, using their seemingly extensive knowledge of the local flora to come up with some sort of poison that might make even a superficial arrow wound lethal. In that case, it would prove to be a dangerous experiment indeed. And I must admit the whole idea scares me. However, if they understood the concept of archery . . . well, given their manual dexterity, that would be merely imitative behavior and in itself might not prove to be a strong case for sentience. But if they applied it in the way I suggested or some variation thereof, that would prove sentience beyond a doubt, wouldn't it? And your work would be done."

"It would put the icing on the cake," said Nils. "Their use of tools and weapons, those seed-pod hurlers in particular, should be enough to prove their sentience. Yet you could teach a chimpanzee to use tools after a fashion."

"But not to *make* tools," said Fannon.

"I don't know. Some amazing work has been done with Terran primates," replied Björnsen. "I'm betting on sentience, myself. At least, I've pretty much taken it for granted by now. But I've still got these unresolved doubts. I'd prefer to take a really strong case back with me to ColCom. If we can establish some level of communication, if we can prove that there's some sort of social structure among the Shades . . ."

"Yes, I see what you mean," said Fannon. "Even Terran primates have a social structure." He snorted. "This is the damnedest case I've ever seen. So many contradictions."

"So? What do you think?"

Fannon pursed his lips. "Okay. Let's try it."

"Colonel?"

Shelby nodded.

That night, feeling somewhat claustrophobic in the small lighter with the two men, Shelby went outside to feel the breeze and watch the crescent-shaped moon. It would rise and set several times during the night, and if she stared at it, she could see it slowly, slowly tumbling. She liked watching it. She could not remember how long it had been since she had stood on *soil* and felt a breeze that did not come from cooling fans. Fannon stepped outside and joined her, keeping his distance and not speaking until he was certain she knew that he was there. He lighted one of his precious, very nonregulation cigarettes.

"Nice night, isn't it?"

"I would guess most of them are, here," she said after a while.

"Would you rather be alone?"

She swallowed. "No. No, please stay. I'm afraid I don't feel very comfortable with you, but maybe if I try . . . I'm just a little worn out, that's all."

"Well, if it makes you feel any better, I feel kinda down myself."

"You?"

She risked a quick glance at him and saw him smile. She looked away. Fannon inhaled on his cigarette and blew a long stream of smoke out into the evening air.

"Yeah, a little. I don't know, I just feel kinda lonely. Sort of crept up on me, I guess. I just wish we could get this survey over with and head back home." He paused, and she thought she heard him mumble the word "home" again under his breath, making a question out of it. "I guess that would be a whole lot easier on you too, eh?"

Shelby raised her eyebrows. This was a side of himself that the very self-sufficient Fannon had not revealed before. She stared out at the perimeter of their camp, then started to walk out toward it slowly. She was aware that he followed.

"Is Björnsen . . . ?"

"Sleeping. He wants to get an early start tomorrow."

Their lighter sat in the clearing which its engines had burned out. The perimeter around it consisted of a Sturmann Field set up around the lighter in a circle, poles planted about fifteen yards apart.

"Nice to have the Sturmann poles," he said. "It makes enjoying the night air possible, thin as it is. You seem to be adjusting to the atmosphere pretty well. Wendy . . .

Lieutenant Chan had a more difficult time with it than we did." He became silent for a short while as they walked the perimeter. He stayed off to one side, so as not to crowd her. "She was too frail for this kind of work."

"She passed the training."

"Simulated training is one thing," he said, "reality's another." He stopped suddenly, his attention caught by something just beyond the field. "Hello—what's this?"

She followed his gaze and saw what looked to be a mass of scattered branches just beyond the Sturmann Field. There were no trees growing anywhere near the field's edge to account for the branches having randomly fallen there that way.

"It would appear that we've had visitors," said Fannon. "At least *a* visitor."

Shelby frowned. "I don't see—"

"Take a good close look at the distribution of those branches," Fannon said, and she saw at once what he meant. "The larger ones are closer to the field's edge than the smaller ones are. The larger they are, the closer they are. The smaller the branches, the farther away. It looks like someone has been *throwing* those branches, possibly some small ones at first, then larger ones progressively, throwing them into the field to see what would happen."

"You mean a Shade?"

He nodded.

"Natural curiosity? Perhaps it saw an animal come up against the field and become stunned. Then it decided to experiment."

"Hmmm, yes. You know, Colonel, I just thought of something. You recall what Nils said about their not perceiving us as a threat?"

"I see what you mean. The field would be a threat, wouldn't it?"

"More than just the field. We saw how seriously they take their territoriality. And we know that they're intimately involved in taking care of their domains. Yet we've been hopping about on their planet, setting our lighter down here and there, burning out clearings for landing zones, very possibly killing some of their game in the process . . ."

"Disrupting the domains of individual Shades, or more

than individuals, if the lighter set down on overlapping territories," she finished for him.

"God, how stupid can you get? Why didn't this occur to any of us before?"

"There's more than enough to think about," she replied. "I didn't understand about the branches until you explained it to me. Don't be too hard on yourself. What we're suffering from is too much input and not enough correlation. The point is, we don't think the same way they do."

"Yeah. To us, we're just burning out a temporary landing zone that will eventually grow over once again. But if I saw something big and strange coming down out of the sky and burning up the garden in my own backyard, I'd probably be pretty frightened. And once I got over my fear, I'd be pretty damn angry. Only they're not afraid of us and they don't seem angry, do they? Why? No teamwork in a nontribal environment?"

"It wouldn't take teamwork for them to react," Shelby said.

"No, of course it wouldn't. If a bunch of people started throwing rocks into a shallow cave where a bear was holed up, there would be just the one bear, but it would come out and charge. They'd be threatening its home."

"Only the Shades don't seem to be doing anything," said Shelby.

Fannon nodded. "They just go about their business, and if they see one of us, it's just 'Oh, look, an alien, ho-hum' and back to whatever they were doing. What's it take to get a rise out of them?"

They stood in silence for a long moment, and Shelby realized suddenly that she had been holding up her own end of the conversation with no more difficulty than she would experience taking care of her duties aboard ship. Had she become so interested that she forgot to feel anxiety in his presence?

"Fannon," she said, "hasn't it struck you that all of us have been . . . well, that we've all been more than a little slow on the uptake here?"

"You mean about our threatening their sense of territoriality?"

"No, much more than that. We have all this information, but we're taking forever to make sense out of it. There has to be something staring us right in the face, only we can't see it for some reason."

"I don't follow."

She felt on the verge of some insight, but it seemed to just keep eluding her. "Have you found that you've been having trouble concentrating lately?"

"What?"

"Concentrating. I don't know, but it seems to me that ever since I set foot on this planet, I've been wandering about in some sort of a semi-fugue state. I've felt that since I left the lighter. Why am I suddenly talking to you like this? It wasn't long ago that just the idea of being in the same room with you and Björnsen made me want to scream. And yet . . . and yet, you have no idea how crazy this seems, but I suddenly don't feel like being alone! It's as if . . . something's missing. I never felt anything like it before. Is it just me? How have you been feeling lately?"

Fannon met her gaze. "A little low."

"And Björnsen?"

"He hasn't been quite himself, either. I know that I've been feeling out of sorts, but I figured what with Wendy coming down with—"

"Coming down with *what*? You still don't know for sure, do you?"

Fannon scowled. "No, I don't. This isn't supposed to happen to people like us. I've been on missions where people have died and it didn't affect me like this. Even with the closeness that develops, you just learn to accept it. It's part of the risk, you know it can happen, and you can't let it interfere with the job."

"*Something's* happening."

"I may be getting paranoid in my old age, but I think you might be right. I feel like I've been walking in my sleep on this mission. We got more accomplished during the first week here than we've done in the last month. That never even occurred to me before."

"I want to get out of here," she said.

Fannon glanced at her sharply. He had said almost exactly the same thing to Nils.

"You know we can't do that," he said. "Unfeeling though it may seem, despite what happened to Wendy, we haven't enough evidence of any danger to the party to justify scrubbing the mission. What do we say when we get back? That one member of the team cracked under the strain and that the rest of us were feeling vaguely uneasy and homesick? That just won't wash with ColCom. We've got to give them hard facts. Still, we'd better go and wake up Nils. If there's anything abnormal in our systems, we've got to find out *now*."

They returned to the same location several days later. Intensive physical examinations by Nils had revealed nothing. They were all in perfect health. They had even checked an additional blood sample from Wendy, one of those taken before they had put her back in coldsleep, but it had shown nothing then and it showed nothing now. There was no change. Everything seemed normal. Before they left, Shelby had stared long and hard at Wendy, asleep in the cryogen. She looked so calm and peaceful.

They had decided to proceed with all available speed, to try to conclude their work as quickly as possible. Returning to the planet surface, they set up camp once again and set about constructing some crude but effective bows from springy saplings, and they cut several dozen arrows, using the feathers from a variety of local flying creature as vanes. They tried to keep their handiwork as close as possible to what they had observed to be the limitations of the natives.

"If one of us finds a Shade, we signal?" Shelby asked.

"If you can elicit a response of some sort, yes," replied Nils. "And don't stray too far. If you see a Shade, get its attention if you can and let it see you shooting at a tree or something. Then just leave the bow and arrows behind and see what it will do. And for God's sake, be careful. You won't have anybody watching your backs, so be wary of the local fauna. Use your weapons if you have to, but avoid killing a Shade under *any* circumstances. Just stun it if there's no other choice and get the hell out of there. And we check in with each other and report progress and location once a minute, on the minute. Is that clear?"

"It's not too late to change our minds," said Shelby.

"No, what the hell, let's do it," said Fannon. "All this uncertainty's getting to me. I can't take it any longer."

They each took a position around the perimeter, between two Sturmann poles. Then, with a final apprehensive look at each other, they each canceled out the field between the two poles where they stood, passed through, reactivated the field and split up, heading into the wild.

Shelby carried the longbow in her left hand, her right hand on her weapon. She kept a steady watch as she walked, and every time she heard the timing bleep of her communicator, she checked in with Nils and Fannon. They tried to stay fairly close to each other, in case trouble should arise. None of them saw any Shades, although Fannon reported dispatching one of the large, feline-looking creatures that they had called pumas, for their resemblance to the extinct Terran animal.

It was a strange feeling for Shelby to be walking through a forest, but she felt preoccupied in spite of her surroundings. It made no sense for Wendy Chan to have gone into such a deep withdrawal for no apparent reason. It was certainly possible that there had been something so deeply buried in her subconscious that the ColCom psych tests hadn't picked it up, but it was highly unlikely. It was far more reasonable to assume that what had happened to her had to do with Boomerang. She thought of the Terran tsetse fly. There was a wide variety of insect life on Boomerang, most of which tended to be considerably larger than Terran insects. However, in the team's research, they had not run across any sort of toxin that would produce a catatonic state in a victim, though that didn't mean that there wasn't one. Besides, there had been no trace of any sort of venom in her system.

Yet they had all admitted feeling a bit depressed, and there was no accounting for it. Both Nils and Fannon had said that they had felt a little maudlin even before Wendy's breakdown, if it was a breakdown. . . . It was out of character for her, it was out of character for Björnsen, and it was especially out of character for Fannon. They were all eminently suited to their work. Nils and Fannon had been doing survey work for many of their biological years; she had been a shuttle pilot before being assigned to voyages of longer duration. Being alone for extended periods of time had never bothered her—it was what she liked. Damm it, she thought, people like us just don't break down!

She suddenly heard a roaring sound and, almost immediately afterward, the sharp report of an exploding seed pod. Then there was a loud thrashing, coming from what seemed to be only several yards to her left, beyond a thick screen of brush. She drew her weapon and pushed through into a small clearing. She fired at the long, sinewy form. It fell to the ground, dead. It was a hellhound, a particularly vicious form of wildlife which Wendy Chan had named for its long and deadly fangs and sharp, talonlike claws. And it had severely mauled a Shade.

It must have surprised the Shade, for it had missed with its seed-pod hurler and obviously had not had time to try anything else. Shelby stared at the poor being, stunned. The Shade had been literally ripped open, and its entrails were hanging out. It was still alive, but dying fast. And there was absolutely nothing she could do to help. It would be a matter of seconds. She knelt down by the gray-skinned being and gently caressed its mane. It looked at her, and there was no expression of pain upon its face, but there was agony in those bright violet eyes that seemed to shimmer. Even as she watched, they began to glaze. Then, for just a moment, they cleared. Slowly, the Shade reached out with one hand and touched her breast, and those gorgeous, tragic eyes locked with hers.

Shelby spoke into her communicator. "Fannon—"

Then she felt a searing blast of pain, like a fireball exploding in her mind.

CHAPTER TWO

They found her just as it was growing dark. By following the signal from her communicator, they had been able to tell that she was moving slowly and erratically, but she was not responding to their calls. She seemed to be in a daze as they brought her back to the lighter. Her clothes were torn and dirty; her face was scratched by branches. Her hair was tangled and wild, and her eyes were wide, staring off into infinity. Other than some minor scratches and bruises, there was nothing wrong with her. Physically.

They immediately lifted off and returned to the ship in orbit around Boomerang.

"We never should have separated," Nils said. "I figured we'd be safe if we remained close by, within reach. . . ."

"Forget it," Fannon said tersely. "Feeling guilty isn't going to solve anything. We all agreed to it. The fault lies as much with myself and Shelby." He glanced at her, sitting in the flight chair, eyes vacant, breathing regularly.

"What do we do now?" asked Nils quietly.

"Abort," said Fannon.

Nils nodded slowly. He looked utterly destroyed.

They took the ship out of orbit and made preparations to put Shelby into coldsleep. They prepared the cryogen right next to Wendy's. They tried not to think about the task ahead of them. They had to bring the ship back home. Both of them were trained for it, but neither of them had piloted a ship for years. One slight error in the computer programming, one mistake in course adjustment . . .

When everything was ready and the ship was under way, Nils approached Shelby and loosened her restraints. He helped her up.

"Come on, Shelby," he said softly. "It's time to go to sleep."

She looked at him, her eyes not quite focusing. She did not resist as he took her hand and led her over to the cryogen. Fannon was waiting to help her in. They picked her up and gently laid her down inside the unit.

"Goodnight, Shelby," Fannon said.

She turned her face to look at him and blinked her eyes several times.

"Take us home," she said.

They sat around the table, Nils and Fannon opposite each other, Shelby between them. Fannon, in a burst of frenetic nicotine activity, had smoked up the rest of his cigarettes, and he drummed his fingers incessantly upon the surface of the table.

"I say we go back," he said.

"And risk another one of us becoming . . . affected?" Nils shook his head. "No way."

"It's our job to take risks, Nils," said Fannon. "Besides, Shelby wasn't affected by whatever it was in quite the same manner as was Wendy. She's not catatonic. She's functional."

"But she's not functioning *normally*," said Nils. "Look at her, for God's sake!"

They both spoke about her as though she weren't even there. In a way, she wasn't. She waited, watching, saying nothing.

"We're not going to learn anything by running away," said Fannon. "We've got a lot at stake here." He stood and started pacing nervously. "Our job's not done. If we can keep Shelby from going under all the way, we might be able to find out what happened. And maybe then we'll be able to help Wendy."

"You're the one who wanted to get out," Nils reminded him. "What happened to change your mind all of a sudden?"

"I don't know. There's something about that place. It

was getting to me. Maybe I panicked. I don't like that. When I start getting spooked that easily, it's time for me to quit. And I'm not ready to quit, goddammit. I feel better now. And I think we should go back and find out what happened. We should finish what we started."

"What about Wendy?"

"All right, what *about* Wendy? There's nothing we can do for her as things stand. The way she is right now, we can go back to ColCom or we can return to Boomerang and it won't make any difference to her either way." He stopped pacing and his lips tightened into a grimace. "At the risk of sounding totally insensitive, Wendy'll keep."

"*Jesus,* Drew . . ."

"Look, I told you that Wendy wasn't as strong as we are. I said she wasn't suited to this kind of work. I'm not being a bastard, Nils, I know what we've got to do. When we had to put Wendy into coldsleep, *you* were the one who realized that ColCom wouldn't recognize that as sufficient grounds to abort the survey. You remember? All right, granted, something's happened to Shelby and neither of us knows what or what to do about it, but *she* wants to go back and I think we should."

"Maybe you're right."

"I *know* I'm right."

"We could be making a very serious mistake."

"Does anybody want to know what my opinion is?" asked Shelby quietly.

They both stopped talking and looked at her. She had changed somehow. Suddenly there was something uncomfortably ethereal about her. She kept vacillating between lucidity and being elsewhere, somehow detached. She seemed dopey.

"We have a responsibility to finish the mission," she said. "I know there's something wrong with me. I'm not sure what's happening. I feel very strange. I know I was completely out of it for a while. That Shade did something to me . . . I'm not sure how. It hurt. It hurt terribly."

"But you show no signs of any injury," said Fannon. "At least, nothing that couldn't be accounted for by your blundering through the underbrush." He didn't say "just like Wendy," although he thought it.

"I *was* hurt," she insisted. "Perhaps they possess a capability for hurting more than the flesh. Some sort of psychic force or something."

"You mean like telepathy?" said Nils. "That might answer a lot of questions, but they're so primitive . . ."

"We want to go back."

Nils leaned forward and stared at her intently. "You keep saying that we should go back. Why? Aren't you frightened?"

Shelby squeezed her eyes shut tightly, then blinked and rubbed them. "I—well, that's what we're here for, isn't it?" She rose to her feet and walked unsteadily to the observation port. The two men exchanged worried looks.

"We go back?" asked Fannon.

Nils took a deep breath and let it out slowly. "We go back."

The lighter set down on the planet's surface while it was still night, but Shelby seemed impatient to get outside. They had to urge her to wait until morning, because the Sturmann Field had to be set up first and they would not risk trying it at night. She acceded to their wishes, but with an obvious display of reluctance. None of them slept during what remained of Boomerang's night.

"She's acting crazy," Fannon said. "She just can't wait to get out there."

"What she said makes sense, though," Nils replied. "If the Shades *are* telepaths, then that would explain a great deal. Maybe it's not even conscious on their part, or fully developed. It could be a strong latent ability of some sort. Wendy might've run into a Shade out there. None of us has had a chance to get very close to them. Except Shelby. We know that for a fact. You and I haven't had the same proximity, but we've felt something . . . a depression, a sense of loneliness completely out of character with our psychological makeup. It's possible that the Shades can project a sort of Sturmann Field of their own without the aid of generators."

"You mean they're trying to repel us by *wishing* us away?" Fannon shook his head. "I can't believe that. Shelby wanted to come back. But you may have a point. What Shelby described feeling when that Shade touched her sounded like it could have been some sort of mind jolt. God, wouldn't that be something? But then why don't they use it on each other if they have that capability? Why fight hand to hand?"

"They have the capability to make hunting weapons," Nils said, "but we haven't seen them using those on each other, either."

"More questions than answers," Fannon said bitterly. "It's like we're right back where we started, and this planet's already got two of us. Or one and a half; I can't decide about Shelby. I don't think she's telling us everything. And I'm not sure whether or not we should confront her with that in her present condition."

"Well, it's going to be dawn soon and she seems to want to go outside very badly. And I want very badly to know why."

"Why not let her?"

"And follow her to see just what she does? She could just start thrashing about in the underbrush again. She keeps vacillating between being rational and disoriented." Björnsen paused, deep in thought. "All right," he said finally, "let's see what happens. But if she goes schizoid or anything like that, I'm for aborting, and this time no turning back."

"Fair enough," said Fannon. "But I'm going to keep a healthy distance from any Shades we run across."

Shelby stepped into the clearing, in full view of the Shade. It was a female and she had a young one with her. They had been sitting on their haunches eating gobfruit when they sensed her presence. The Shade had glanced up sharply, rising to her feet and staring at where Shelby had stood among the trees. Shelby squeezed past the narrow boles of the tall and slender saplings. The Shade didn't move. Shelby came several steps closer, then stopped. There was none of that passive acceptance they had seen so often from other Shades. Shelby definitely had this one's attention. The Shade took one step forward, then hesitated. Slowly, the Shade put down its weapons, laying them carefully on the ground.

"It's going to attack her!" whispered Fannon. He held his weapon at the ready.

"Maybe not," said Nils. "Let's wait and see."

Shelby hadn't moved. Neither had the Shade. For a long moment, they both simply stood there, staring at each other. Then a strange look passed over the Shade's features. It inclined its head to one side in a very human-seeming gesture, then started to step forward again, but stopped. It seemed confused.

Shelby took one step to the side, then stopped. Then she started swaying unsteadily. Fannon almost jumped into the clearing, but in another moment Shelby turned and bolted back the way she had come. The Shade continued to stare after her for a long time, even after it had returned to squat by its child.

They returned to the lighter, Shelby walking with confidence through the forest, remaining silent all the way. She seemed very much at home all of a sudden. The men had to struggle to keep up with her, and they were in better physical condition than she was. When they entered the lighter, Shelby sat down and placed her hands over her eyes.

"What happened out there, Shelby?" Nils asked anxiously. "What is it? Are you all right?"

"We were meant to challenge," she said vaguely, "but I couldn't do it. We started to initiate the ritual, but I just couldn't go through with it."

"What are you talking about?" said Fannon. "You wanted to *challenge* that Shade?"

She looked up at him, and Fannon saw that her eyes were wild.

"I don't know how to make you understand," she said. "I'm not just Shelby Michaels anymore."

She saw Fannon look at Nils, and she shook her head.

"It isn't what you think." She laughed suddenly and there was no mirth in the sound. "I'm not going crazy. We are not insane." She leaned back and exhaled heavily. She massaged her temples slowly, a glazed look in her eyes. "It's absolutely incredible. I don't know how—I just don't know what to say. It's frightening."

"You're not making sense," said Nils. He licked his lips nervously. "What happened? Did that Shade do—"

"No, it's nothing like that," she said. "They're not telepathic. I thought so too, at one point. Even before my encounter with that dying Shade, I had started to think that perhaps they might communicate on some telepathic level. It didn't make any sense for them to live that way and not ever communicate with each other, but that's just it, they *don't*. That's why they don't have any form of tribal structure—they have no need of one."

"I don't understand," said Nils.

"Why talk to others when you can talk to yourself?" said Shelby with a strange smile.

"Look, this is no time for guessing games," said Fannon. "Nils, I think we'd best get out of here. She's not well."

"I don't think she's being irrational," said Nils slowly.

"I'm as clear-headed as I've ever been," said Shelby. "I'm remembering so many things! Things I never even knew." She looked from one man to the other. "It's finished. The mission, I mean. I can supply all the missing information, all the details. And there can only be one conclusion. Boomerang is not suitable for colonization. Oh, it could very easily be colonized, but we'd destroy them. We'd upset the entire balance of this planet. The Shades would never be able to adapt.

"My mind was a sort of blank for a while. It was like feeling all . . . dizzy inside. It all seems to be coming together, but I don't know if I can handle it. God, it scares the shit out of me."

Both men sat down. Neither said a word.

"When I came upon that Shade, the wounded one, I knew that he was dying. And I was sick at the thought that there was nothing I could do to help him. I knew that in a few seconds he'd be gone. I had no idea what he was feeling. He didn't seem to be in pain . . . at least, he wasn't reacting the way a human would react or an animal. There was no outward sign of his *feeling* the hurt. I didn't even know if I could be of any comfort, but something made me want to try."

She knelt down by the gray-skinned being and gently caressed its mane. It was still alive, but dying fast. And there was absolutely nothing she could do to help. It would be a matter of seconds. It looked at her and there was agony in those violet eyes that seemed to shimmer. Even as she watched, they glazed. Then, for just a mo-

ment, they cleared. Slowly, the Shade reached out with one hand and touched her breast, those gorgeous tragic eyes locked with hers. And then Shelby felt a searing blast of pain, like a fireball exploding in her mind.

She tried to recoil from the contact, but found that she could not. It seemed that they were somehow riveted together. Then, suddenly, it was over and she fell back upon the ground, clutching at her head. It felt as if someone had inserted a burning needle deep into her skull. She thrashed around on the forest floor, spasming with pain. She was beyond screaming. It was more than she could possibly absorb, and the brain sought retreat in oblivion, but there was no escape from the churning of thousands of images, from fleeting glimpses of alien realities, from ancient memories—

A Shade was bending over her. Her eyes opened and she looked at him. He straightened and backed away a step, a strange look upon his face, a look of understanding and of pain. She wondered how she could see it. Slowly, in a daze, she sat up and watched as the Shade stooped over the inert body of the other. He gazed at the slain being with what seemed like longing, then he turned and stared at her once more, fearfully. Then there was the sound of footsteps approaching noisily and rapidly. The Shade melted away into the forest.

She didn't remember getting to her feet. When she was aware of what was happening around her once again, she was in a different place and she was walking, but she was breathing heavily, as though she had been running for quite some distance.

Everything began to look familiar. She stopped and stared at a blighted tree that she had healed. She recalled picking the berries from the bush just ten feet away and mashing them into a pulp running with dark juice, then burying the crushed berries at the roots of the young sapling, knowing that the trace elements would help the tree to heal. It was coming along well; almost no trace of the blight remained. A short while later, she found herself drawn to a spot that she seemed to know. And she remembered it. It was there that she had successfully challenged for domain, many years ago, even before she had been born. She remembered painstakingly making her first jave-

lin and narrowly escaping with her life when the giant mothlike creature stung her. She had slit her arm to remove the sting, then applied climbing moss to the wound. She had been feverish for many days, but she had survived.

It was an unceasing flow of remembrance. The sluice gates opened and generations of experience washed over her like a flood. When they found her, wandering about in her domain, savoring, remembering, she almost walked away from them. They seemed so . . . alien.

"Nils," she said, "do you recall when you said that we don't fit into their experience? If you could only conceive of just how right you were! We don't correspond to *anything* in their experience. And not only because we're human and they're not. They have no concept of individuality. They simply can't even begin to relate to it because none of them are individuals, really. That's why they have no need of communication, no need for any form of tribal society. Each Shade is his *own* tribe. Each Shade is a culture, a civilization. Each Shade is a world.

"They can't die. Imagine what death would be like if not only *you* were to die, but at the same time every friend and ancestor that you've ever had. Not the death of one, the death of hundreds, thousands! A Shade can't die alone. When the time comes, a sort of signal is sent out . . . a call . . . and one responds and there is a . . . merging. The one I came upon and saved from being devoured knew that he was dying and he had sent out the call, but he also knew that the respondent wouldn't arrive in time. What he must have gone through in those last few seconds, trying to decide between the dying out of an entire line and passing on to me, an alien! But the drive . . . the sheer respect for life won out, and he merged with me.

"It's tearing me apart. I'm a human, I'm Shelby Michaels, and yet I'm all of *them* as well. It's confusing and it's frightening and—I'm aware of them inside me, on the edge of my consciousness. Sometimes it feels like they're there, more dominant, and then they seem to go away, I can't make out—"

"Shelby," Nils said gently, "you're one of *us*."

She shook her head. "Not anymore. There's much more

to it than that. You don't know what I'm going through. To the Shades, we seem so unbelievably tragic, so alone, they just can't bear to be in contact with us. That's what must have happened to Wendy. She was very sensitive. Her files said that she had latent esper potential. What Wendy must have picked up on must have been an unconscious projection of how they perceive us, and suddenly the encapsulation, the entombment, in her own ego must have hit her so hard, through their eyes, that she just couldn't take it. She fled from her loneliness in the only way she could."

"Shelby, Wendy can be helped," said Fannon. "We can get you help, too. You're right, we don't know what you're going through, we have no way of knowing, but now that the mission is over, now that we know what we needed to know, we can go home."

"I *can't*," she said. There were tears in her eyes. "The instinct that this is my home is so overwhelming. . . . A part of me thinks of a ship as being home, but so many other parts of me know Boomerang as home."

"Are you saying you want us to *leave* you here?" asked Nils.

"I don't know. God, I'm so tired. I can barely keep my eyes open. I'm getting a terrible headache."

"I think we'd better sedate you so you can get some rest," said Nils.

"You think I'm crazy, don't you?" she said.

"No one said you're crazy," he replied. "But you're exhausted. And we need to think about what you've just told us."

"You're not going to put me into coldsleep."

"No, I'm just going to administer a mild sedative. You do trust me, don't you?"

"All right. Do whatever you think you must. I just can't take it anymore. My head feels like it's going to burst. Just put me out so I don't have to deal with it for a while. But please, not coldsleep."

"I won't do anything you don't want me to do," he said. "Drew, get me the medpak, will you?" He picked up her hand to take her pulse. She seemed very weak after talking to them, and she was flushed with perspiration. She closed her eyes.

After they had placed her, sedated, onto a bunk, they sat drinking coffee together.

"Do you believe all that?" asked Fannon.

"You mean do I think it's a psychosis?" He shrugged. "How the hell am I supposed to know? It *sounds* believable."

"Psychotics are supposed to be good at that, aren't they?"

Nils did not respond.

"I never knew that Wendy had latent esper potential," said Fannon.

"You never had access to her files."

"She could have just made that up, you know. Wendy went catatonic. Maybe Shelby freaked out in her own way. Manufactured some sort of reality to explain what had happened to her."

"If she did make it all up, what *really* happened?"

Fannon sighed. "I *want* to believe it. And I'm afraid to believe it."

"If we accept that what she told us is what really happened," said Nils, "then we've got the answers to all our questions. Only now we've got a whole new list of questions, don't we?"

"God, I hate this mission."

Nils nodded and took a long sip from his coffee bulb. He put it down, empty. "I believe her," he said.

"If you do believe her, what are you going to do about it? A psychosis is a hell of a lot easier to treat than a merging with some sort of multiple alien personality."

Nils covered his face with his hands, leaning his elbows on the table. His fingers clutched at his scalp. He shook his head in resignation.

"God knows. I can't do anything for her. I don't know if anyone can. This entire mission has turned into a disaster. We got all our answers, but at what cost? What else can we do? Put her into coldsleep and get back somehow, let ColCom take over? I don't envy them their task. And I feel for her. What are they going to do? Quarantine her. Put her under observation, pump her full of drugs; how the hell can you cure somebody of an alien invasion right into the core of their identity? That's assuming *they* believe her story. How can she prove it?"

"You're forgetting something else," said Fannon. "She's a pilot. She's been alone for most of her adult life. It almost turned her inside out just trying to establish some sort of a rapport with us, and even that wasn't very close. She's put up an awful lot of shields to keep people out. Unless this is some sort of a psychosis she developed because contact with us was more than she could handle, she's going to have to deal with contact with an alien race on the most intimate level imaginable. All her barriers won't help her now—they're already inside."

"I didn't forget about that," Nils said wearily. "I just didn't want to think about it."

"What worries me," said Fannon, "is that if we're going to accept her story at face value, then these Shade . . . ancestors or whatever you want to call them are a part of her somehow, on the edge of her consciousness, she said. What does that mean exactly? What *is* she going through? Is she just the inheritor of a whole new set of racial memories, or are there actual alien personas inside her now? And if that's the case, then how are *they* going to handle contact with her when just being physically near us bothers them? And what happens if they become dominant?"

"It's a horrifying thought," said Nils.

"I hate to say this," Fannon said, his face grim, "but I hope to God she's flipped out."

Nils Björnsen snorted bitterly. "Yeah, how about that? If she's become psychotic, then the mission is a failure, but there may be some hope for her. But if she's not crazy, if that incredible story is true, then the mission is a success. And if that's the case, then how can she possibly hope to hang onto her sanity?"

"And just how sane are pilots anyway?"

It had finally been said. Since Shelby had revived, both men had wondered which of them would be the first to actually come out and say it.

"Either way, we don't really have much choice, do we?" Björnsen said. "We've done as much as we could here. It's not our ballgame anymore."

"I agree. And there's no question about trusting Shelby to get us back. We don't dare let her near that computer. Whether she likes it or not, it's coldsleep for her."

"You mean right away? I don't know, Drew, maybe we could—"

"Maybe we could what? Let the sedative wear off and risk her flipping out even more? I don't really want to deal with that."

"You're convinced she's imagining all this, aren't you?"

"I'm not convinced of anything. At this point, neither you nor I can afford to take anything on faith, Nils. That's not our job. Shelby isn't our responsibility anymore. Her usefulness as a pilot, at least in her present condition, is clearly over. From now on, whatever's to be done about Shelby and Wendy is a case for ColCom, not for us. We've got more than enough to worry about. When's the last time you piloted a ship?"

Nils grimaced. "During training."

"Yeah. You see my point? We can't afford any more time for Shelby. We've got our hands full as it is."

"I know, but I gave her my word."

"Sure you did. But is it worth your life? She's your patient, Nils. At least until you can get her back to where they can take proper care of her. You gave her your word, you set her mind at ease—doctors do it all the time, man. Chalk it up to bedside manner and let's get on with it, okay? The sooner we get underway, the better I'll like it."

"I suppose you're right."

"You know I'm right. This damn planet has turned us into noodles. I wouldn't be surprised if they put us into analysis when we get back. I've seen raw recruits who could handle a mission better than we've handled this one."

Nils nodded. "We've made some bad mistakes. They're not going to go easy on us."

"No, they certainly won't. But let's take one thing at a time, shall we? Right now the first order of business is to get back to the ship. We've got a lot of equipment out there to load up and the Sturmann Field to take down, and it's all got to get finished before dark. And if I never see this place again, it'll be just fine with me."

"All right, but I want to check on Shelby once again. If we're going to keep her under until we're ready to put her into coldsleep, I'm going to have to administer a stronger sedative."

They got up and went into the other cabin of the lighter, where they had put Shelby to rest. The moment they opened the hatch that separated the two compartments, they knew something was wrong. They felt a breeze. The bunk where Shelby had lain was empty. And the emergency escape hatch of the lighter was wide open. It had been opened manually, so that the explosive charges that were set into the hatch to blow it open would not have alerted them. Shelby was gone. And her communicator was lying on the bunk.

There was no way to track her.

CHAPTER THREE

The time was almost come, he could feel it. The Ones Who Were could feel it too, and he was aware of their restlessness. Soon the Need would be upon them all and it would be time to journey to the mountains once again. Time to set aside the hunting and the caring, time to set aside the lives that are and those that were for the lives that will one day be. Time for the mating.

The One That Is knew that now was the time to hunt well. It was the time for the body to become fortified so that the long journey would not be an arduous one, for once the Need came upon them, there would be no time for hunting. No time for eating or for sleeping. There would only be the Need. And when that time came, they would journey to the mating ground with all their beings filled by the Need and all their minds set upon the destination. They would think of nothing else. And they would stop for nothing. They could not.

The One That Is had only seen one time of Need before, and now that memory came flooding back to him. He remembered his first mating dance and his first coupling, and the memory filled him with warm pleasure.

"The One That Is felt hunger and uncertainty, as it always is with the very young. When the Need arrives, there is the urge to fall upon the first female that comes in sight, but that is not the Way. That is the Way of beasts, and the people are not beasts. The Need is good, but the Ritual is greater. The Need is but the means. The Ritual is the definition. The Ritual is the Way. It is reaffirmation, and it reminds us of the meaning of our lives. It is always a time of joy for the Great Father, for it is the Great Father who must guide the body and the soul of the One That Is so that the Ones Who Were can all remember and take part."

"As it is the role of the Great Hunter to instruct and guide the One That Is in all the ways of killing and providing. The Great Hunter is no less important. I am the one who must guide the body and the soul of the One That Is so that the time of Need does not blind him to the dangers of the journey. I am the one who must remember that the time of Need is not the time to challenge. The Great Father is the one who brings the wisdom, but it is the Great Hunter who provides the spirit!"

"The One That Is respects the wisdom and the spirit," said R'yal, but not aloud, "but the One That Is would like to guide the body and the soul during this mating. The One That Is is older now and wiser and he remembers that first mating. The One That Is knows and understands the Ritual."

"R'yal, the One That Is, has greater wisdom now and spirit, true, but the One That Is is young yet."

"Not so young he is incapable of guiding."

"A young beast can guide itself, R'yal," the Great Mother told him, "but it has no ancestors on whom it can depend for wisdom and for sureness. It can only learn by doing, not by what was done. And such a learning process brings with it great risk and pain."

"The One That Is has no fear of risk and pain."

"Hah! No fear of risk? No fear of pain? What happened, then, when the One That Is received the Call? Why was there no merging?"

The Ones That Were all suddenly turned silent. Even the Great Hunter, with his brashness, made known his regret at having spoken of that which none of them could bear to remember.

R'yal had hurried to the merging when he received the Call. He trusted to the Hunter to protect him and he knew that the Great Father would grant him the wisdom to find the way to where the fallen one was waiting, but it was he who had to guide the merging. That was the Way. It always has to be the One That Is who merges, the One That Is must bear the Touch and feel the pain. The One That Is must *feel* it so that he can grow stronger and wiser, and can understand. But the fallen one was not approachable. The fallen one had already Touched and merged.

Kneeling beside the fallen one was One Who Was Not. The One Who Was Not had felt the Touch. And the Ones That Were that had been with the fallen one were now with One Who Was Not. It was the most terrifying thing that any of them had ever known.

How was it possible? How was it possible to *be* and not *have been*? How could such creatures exist? They were like beasts, but in some ways they resembled people. And they did not act like beasts. There had never been anything like the Ones Who Were Not before.

R'yal did not know where the Ones Who Were Not came from. Not even the Great Father knew, though the Great Father was the oldest and the wisest of the Ones That Were. One day, the Ones Who Were Not simply appeared out of nowhere. And they sought the people. But they *were not*. How could beings who appeared to act like people and who bore a sort of aspect like the people live with such aloneness? How could they be guided? They were beasts, and yet they were not beasts. They were something different, something in between.

R'yal thought of the All Father, and the Ones That Were paid silent homage with him. It was the All Father who made the plants to grow and the game to be plentiful. It was the All Father who tested them to see if they were worthy. And it was the All Father who gave them the seed, who brought on the Need, and who breathed the spirit and the soul into the bellies of the females where the Ones That Will Be grew. But these new creatures were not from the All Father. They were a blasphemy. They shared none of the Way, they knew not the Rituals, they did not Touch and they could not merge. They lived and yet they *were not*. They were evil. They were alien. And they were to be pitied. They did not know the bounty and the presence, the All Father had not breathed his spirit into them. How could they survive the sadness and the pain?

One day, R'yal had seen a great and monstrous creature, the like of which he'd never seen before, a creature the like of which none of the Ones That Were had ever seen before. This strange and awful creature sat immobile in an open space where nothing lived, and the Ones Who Were Not walked into its hungry maw. R'yal and the Ones Who Were had felt great sadness for the blasphemous creatures. Indeed, it seemed that they could *not* survive their sorry state, and so they gave themselves up to be eaten rather than continue as they were. And then the monstrous beast roared terribly, breathed flame and somehow flew up into the sky, even though it had no wings! And the Great Father, in his wisdom, said that the strange beast had been sent by the All Father to end the misery of the pathetic creatures who were not. They were a blight upon the world, and the monster came to make things pure again. But then, to their astonishment, the monster returned to the place where nothing lived and it vomited the creatures out. And R'yal saw that the Ones Who Were Not were so unclean, were such a blasphemy, that not even a beast sent by the All Father could consume them. And he felt afraid.

They were frightening, these creatures who were not. These beasts who walked like people. They could make beasts die merely by pointing at them! And they so polluted the land they claimed that nothing could grow there and no beast could approach it. R'yal had seen one of the beasts set foot upon the place where nothing grew, the land claimed by the Ones Who Were Not, and the beast had howled in agony and been thrown back! And R'yal had wondered if the presence of the Ones Who Were Not had caused the All Father to remove his blessing from that land, so he had broken branches from the trees created by the All Father and tried to throw them upon the land where nothing grew, and the branches would not land! They were thrown back, just as the beast had been! And the Great Mother had been frightened and she said that the All Father had cursed the place where the Ones Who Were Not chose to suffer. The poor creatures tried to die again and again, yet every time they gave themselves up to the flying monster, it soon spat them out again.

"They must live in constant suffering, that they should

try to end their lives with every day," the Great Mother had said. And the Great Father had taken the body and the soul away from that foul place, because the sadness of the cursed creatures was more than they could bear.

And now, horror of horrors, the Ones That Were of the fallen one were with One Who Was Not. How could they possibly survive? How could they flourish within creatures who were so blasphemous that they could not bear to live? How great their agony must be! And R'yal felt pain and guilt because he had let it happen. He had not come in time when it had been his duty. And Great Father T'ran and Great Mother N'lia felt his pain as theirs. Great Hunter D'val raged against the blasphemy because he could not slay it. Great Healer S'eri felt helpless because, with all his knowledge of the Way, he could effect no cure. H'lai, Father Who Walked in Shadow, was furious because with all his fierce will to live, with all his closeness to the beasts, he was helpless in this tragedy. And T'arok and L'yal, Father and Mother of his flesh, felt shame because it was R'yal who had allowed the awful thing to happen.

"It is a thing of sadness and of horror," the Great Father said. "It is a thing that cannot be. We shall be cursed by the All Father if we cannot end this blasphemy."

And there the Great Father stopped, for not even T'ran knew how to end it when the Ones Who Were Not could not be approached. And all the Ones Who Were grew silent, because they shared the guilt. They shared the fear and the desolation. And because the time of Need was almost upon them and nothing could be done. They were all afraid because the time of Need was a time for reaffirmation of the Way and they had failed in their duty. They were afraid that for this the All Father might punish them by not breathing the spirit and the soul into the children of their flesh. But the time of Need was there and nothing could be done. R'yal lay down upon the ground and let the body and the soul be guided by D'val, so that they would be safe. He lay down upon the ground to be closer to the All Father, who made all things to grow. And, with Great Hunter D'val watching, with H'lai Who Walked in Shadow sensing all around them, R'yal and the Ones Who Were began the Ritual of Prayer. They prayed for guidance and for knowledge. They prayed that the flesh of R'yal, the One That Is, would be made fertile. They prayed for a good mating. They prayed for the beasts and all the plants in their domain.

And they prayed for forgiveness.

Shelby felt as if she was falling. There was nothing but space all around her and she was being sucked down and down, spinning into some great void beyond reach of anyone or anything. She knew it was a dream and she struggled to wake up, fought for consciousness with all her being. And she felt herself being pulled along. She felt a strange new strength she didn't know she had. And even deep within her dream, she sensed that she was lying down upon a bunk and she felt its hardness beneath her. She felt more sure of her surroundings, and her fear abated because she knew that she was about to reawaken. Nils had kept his word. She had not been placed in coldsleep.

Then she was standing on her feet inside the lighter, feeling slightly dizzy and uncoordinated. Still on the verge of consciousness. Trying to shrug off the remaining sleepiness, the pulling of the dream. She saw the escape hatch and suddenly she became filled with the overwhelming need to flee.

I must get away, she thought. I must get away and go where they can't find me. I must go home.

She opened the escape hatch manually, so as not to alert Björnsen and Fannon, then she jumped lightly to the ground, still feeling groggy, still feeling halfway between dreaming and reality. She had left her communicator on the bunk, so that the two men would not be able to track her signal and bring her back to be put to sleep again. But she took along with her the nullifier that would allow her to escape past the Sturmann Field. She ran quickly to the edge of the perimeter, vaguely wondering how she could move so well when she felt so dissociated, then she deactivated a portion of the field and slipped past the perimeter. Once outside, she reactivated the field, then dropped the now useless nullifier. She had no intention of returning.

She jogged through the forest, feeling lightheaded and

surefooted. She felt comfortable, exhilarated, refreshed . . . *free.* And she seemed to know where she was going.

And then she realized that *she* didn't know. *They* did.

"Do you believe it now?" asked Björnsen.

He and Fannon, carrying supply packs and weapons, moved through the forest slowly, following her trail. It was a difficult job. If it wasn't for the fact that Drew Fannon had grown up in Colorado and had spent most of his life being an outdoorsman, they would not have had a chance of finding the direction she had taken. Fannon was an expert tracker, and even he had to admit that it was a hard trail to follow. Finding the point where she had entered the forest had been easy enough. They had discovered the nullifier she had dropped once she got beyond the Sturmann Field. But from there on, the going got difficult.

"I don't know what I believe," said Fannon, stooping to check the ground.

"Come on, Drew. Shelby's never been out in the field. She's no good in the woods. By rights, she should have plowed through this country leaving a trail that a blind man could follow. But she didn't, did she? How do you explain it?"

"I'm through trying to explain things," Fannon answered irritably. "I'm through fucking up on this goddam mission. From now on, if I don't *see* it, I don't *buy* it. If I can't sink my teeth into it, it ain't real. We're supposed to be pros at this, and we've handled everything like a couple of rookies that should've flunked out of training. If we're lucky enough to get back, ColCom is going to hand our asses to us."

"What makes you think they care, Drew?" Nils wiped his brow and adjusted his pack. "We're on our own out here. The rules are there just for the sake of there being rules. You have to improvise on every mission. Most of it is guesswork, and a hell of a lot of it is luck. You should know that as well as I do. All ColCom cares about is the answer to one question and one question only: Can the world be colonized? Everything else is secondary."

"Really? Then how come we're tracking Shelby? Because we need our pilot? Is that all there is to it? How come we've been wracking our brains about the Shades, damn them to hell? We had the answer to that one-and-only question a month ago. Are you trying to convince me or yourself?"

Björnsen remained silent for a minute, then he sighed. "Myself, I guess."

"You called it, partner."

They moved on slowly, Fannon's eyes scanning the ground and the underbrush for any signs of Shelby's trail. "You're right about one thing, though," he said. "ColCom doesn't really care."

"How's that?"

"You ever been on a real terror that required extensive debriefing? One of those missions where everything went wrong?"

"You mean like this one?"

"Funny. Yeah, like this one."

"No, never anything quite so bad. Most of my debriefings have been the standard two-week torture sessions."

Fannon snorted. "You've been lucky. They put me through the wringer for a month and a half after the Rhiannon mission."

Björnsen's eyes grew wide. "*You were on Rhiannon?* You never told me that."

"I don't like to talk about it. Maybe if you get me good and drunk one of these days—that's if we survive this fiasco—I'll tell you all about it. You bring the thorazine. That one was supposed to be a real picnic. Only it didn't turn out that way. We didn't lose anyone, thank God, but it wasn't for Rhiannon's lack of trying. Hell, you've heard the stories."

"Some."

"Not from anybody who was there, I'll bet."

"No. Scuttlebutt."

Fannon nodded. "I figured as much. So far as I know, I'm the only one who elected to stay in the service after that. And it wasn't 'cause I love this work that much. Part of it was because I just don't belong anywhere else. And the other part of it was ColCom. Fucking bunch of hypocrites. All that lip service about respect for alien life forms doesn't amount to a hill of beans. It's all hype for the unwashed masses dying to emigrate. When they get on those giant colony ships for the big one-way trip, it helps to know that the place you're going to is going to welcome you with open arms. If we hadn't cared about the Shades, we could have gone back and said, sure, the world is habitable, it's a regular paradise. There *is* this native life form and they do kinda look like people, but they're just animals, don't worry about them. If they get in the way, it's okay to just brush them aside. They don't count for anything. And ColCom would accept that. Somebody else could come along and prove us wrong, but it wouldn't make a bit of difference. They'd have our report and the ship would be sent out and if it turned out that a benevolent, sentient race was wiped out so a bunch of pioneer types could have a place to put up their log cabins, well, tough luck. It wasn't ColCom's fault. They could only act on information they were given at the time. You think that it would bother them? Not in the least.

"But we'd get pulled back from wherever we'd been sent to and they'd throw the book at us and cashier us from the service. And those button pushers at ColCom would be satisfied that they'd done the right thing. That the matter had been taken care of. They'd be absolved of guilt by pinning the whole thing on the survey team.

"But if a sentient race was wiped out and nobody but ColCom was the wiser, guess what? Business as usual. The natives of Rhiannon were as hostile as they come, but the planet was such a desirable piece of real estate that the powers that be were ready to commit genocide just to secure a colony. And the natives of Rhiannon, hostile though they were, were *sentient!* You know why they spent all that extra time debriefing us? They were trying to decide whether or not wiping out the Rhiannans would be cost-effective. *Cost-effective!* So help me.

"Somebody's got to play God. ColCom's not particularly interested in the job. So they look for people like you and me, assholes like us who'll put everything on the line to make that little extra effort, to make the right decision. Not because they have any sort of moral attitude about it, but because the right decisions save them catching flak if it turns out that colonists are forced to inconvenience—yeah, that's actually the word they used when they tried to explain it to a very indignant yours truly—*inconvenience* the locals." Fannon spat upon the ground. "Bastards. They don't care. But *someone's* got to."

Nils was astonished. Then, after a short while, he smiled, though Fannon didn't see it.

"By God, Drew, you're an idealist."

Fannon turned around to see if he was being mocked. When he saw that he wasn't, he scowled, then smiled.

"Yeah, I guess I am. But if you ever tell anyone, I'll bust your jaw."

Nils made a show of looking about him. "Who's there to tell?"

Fannon chuckled. Then he grew serious. "Remind me again that I'm an idealist if we run across any of those Shades. I'll be real tempted to burn 'em for what they did to Wendy. And to Shelby."

"So you *do* believe her," Björnsen said.

"I believe that we're not following a pilot. I don't know if you've noticed it or not, but this trail has been getting harder and harder to follow. Fewer and fewer signs. Almost as though the person that we're tracking started out as a kid who was fairly at home in the woods and has grown up into one hell of an experienced outdoorsman by the time we've come this far. If this keeps up progressively, we're sunk. I'm having a devil of a time as it is."

Fannon sat down on the ground and shifted the weight of his pack. Nils stood watch, his weapon ready in case some beast should come upon them.

"I'm bushed," said Fannon. "This tracking is hard work. I sure am glad my daddy taught me well. The skill's come in handy before, but I've never needed it as much as I do now. It's getting really tough to notice the signs. Looks like they're becoming more and more dominant or aware or something as she moves on."

"Looks like you might be right," agreed Nils. "But there's something that you missed."

"What?"

"Don't you realize where we are?"

"Look, friend, I'm in no mood for riddles. If there's something I should know, you'd better tell me."

"We're in the same general area where we lost Shelby last time. It wasn't too far from here that she ran into that dead Shade we found when we responded to her call. At least that's the way it looks from the compass bearings I've been logging."

Fannon smacked his forehead. "Jesus! If I had any doubts about her story, they're gone now. She's gone back to 'her' domain!"

"If we lose the trail, we can keep searching this area. Chances are she'll stick around here somewhere, unless she deviates from standard Shade behavior."

"Yeah. That's *if* she doesn't deviate from standard Shade behavior. That's *if* she hasn't gone nuts from having strange creatures in her brain. That's *if* she hasn't bought it. She didn't take a weapon with her. And that's *if* I'm wrong about the signs."

Nils frowned. "What do you mean if you're wrong about the signs?"

Fannon sighed heavily. He rose to his feet and dusted himself off, brushing bits of leaves and dry grass off his clothing. "The way it looks to me, partner, Shelby's changed direction. Abruptly."

"What do you mean?"

"She was heading in a southeasterly direction. Here, it looks like she's turned and headed north all of a sudden."

"But to the north—"

"We've got the mountains. And if she gets that far, finding her is going to be a real bitch. What's more, it's going to get dark real soon. And I can't follow this trail in the dark. We're going to have to camp."

"Which will leave the trail that much colder," Nils said.

Fannon nodded. "I'm real ecstatic about that. Cheer up, it could get worse."

"How?"

"It might rain."

CHAPTER FOUR

She recognized her old domain. This was her land, the land that she had claimed, challenged for and won. She giggled and felt herself to be on the edge of hysterics.

My land? *Their* land, not mine. She desperately tried to hold onto Shelby. But it was becoming very hard to do. Shelby was a pilot and her home was the control room of a ship, the console of a ship's computer. But as she moved through the forest, driven by an urge clearly not her own, a feeling of belonging to the soil welled up inside her. She found herself responding to the savage beauty of Boomerang. She liked the feel of the earth and of the moss underneath her feet. She reveled in the splendor of the forest.

The tall trees and the narrow young saplings with their furry bark and blue-green foliage, the strangely beautiful plants that seemed half tree, half bush, a curious bole that curved with the smaller branches growing on the inside, facing up and reaching for the light, the flowering grass, with its yellow blades and purple blooms—all of these were known to her.

She heard the shrill cry of a bird, and though she could not see it, she could picture it clearly in her mind. She recognized the tracks of a hellhound, tracks that Shelby never would have seen, and she knew how long it had been since the animal had passed. And it was not a hell-hound, as the survey team had called them, but a Rhann.

And she heard the strange new name inside her mind, sounded out in a throaty sort of way that sounded much like the roar of the animal itself. And there were other images and words that kept swimming to the forefront of her mind, as well. Some she seemed to understand and some she didn't. And she couldn't shake that groggy, dreamy sort of feeling that she had had when she woke up, the feeling that she wasn't fully conscious, even though she was. There were conflicting emotions in her mind that she could not identify with Shelby, and she was aware of all of them, although she did not truly feel them. She was aware of fear, great fear, and she was aware of sadness. She was aware of pain, but she did not feel it. And she was aware of a sense of great determination and of effort. She felt a power of *will* that was not hers, and she kept thinking of her father, but not *her* father. Not the man who died when she was young and left her all alone; no, there was no sense of that man whatsoever. Rather, there was a strong impression of some paternal force, of age and wisdom. And even though she was not religious, she sensed the concept of a god. *The* God. The Creator of all things, a Druidic sort of entity associated with the soil and fertility . . . the All Father.

She felt like a marionette, her strings being manipulated by some guiding force. She was still loping along at an easy trot even though she had long passed the limits of her endurance, and she felt tears streaming from her eyes. She felt her lungs bursting and her muscles aching, and she wondered how long they could go on pushing her, forcing her to put one foot before the other. At some point, her body had to quit in protest and collapse from the abuse. She wanted to scream from pain and terror, but she felt those emotions somehow being soothed, and an image of her mother flashed before her, a sense of being cared for and protected. But the mother that she felt within her was not a human being.

Finally, she could simply go no farther. And as if the strings were cut, she crumpled to the ground. She dragged herself to lie atop a patch of moss. She felt its thick and woolly texture against her cheek as she lay prone, her muscles jerking, her breaths coming in sobs.

"No more," she moaned, "no more, oh, please, I just can't bear it! Leave me alone! Oh, *please* leave me alone!"

It was dark. The night had fallen, and somewhere up above her, not visible through the trees, the moon of Boomerang tumbled lazily across the sky. Also, somewhere above her, there was the ship. *Her* ship. And she despaired of ever seeing it again. She was exhausted and she had to rest. They could drive her no farther. The forest became full of the noises of the night, and she knew that if she went to sleep, she would most likely die. It was amazing she had made it this far. As a pilot, she had visualized her death in a hundred different ways, but she had never thought that she would quit life upon the surface of an alien world. It's just as well, she thought. How hard can it be? She closed her eyes and fell instantly asleep.

She remembered being born.

She recalled seeing light for the very first time and being unafraid. The mother and the father of her flesh were with her, and she was a part of them as they were a part of her. She was born aware, feeling their pride and love, and she was happy. She was not an empty vessel, waiting to be filled, for there was already a bond between her and the parents of her flesh. N'tral and L'nai were part of her; she had become the One That Is, given life through the blessings of the All Father. Within a short time, she understood that spiritual link with the parents of her flesh. And though N'tral would leave soon after the birthing, she would always feel his presence deep within her. Many years later, when the time came for the body of N'tral to die, his Call was answered by another and the link was broken, his presence slipped away forever. She was not lonely and she did not grieve, for by that time she had already merged and the rapport she felt with her Great Father was stronger by far than the bond she shared with the father of her flesh.

She knew a language older than time itself, a language that had been spoken eons ago, but now was shared only in thought with the Ones Who Were. She grew strong and learned the Way and knew the Rituals, guided by the mother of her flesh, L'nai. For L'nai, there would never be another such as her, for although the people could mate many times, there could only be one blessed birthing, after which the Need was never felt again.

She learned that L'nai and N'tral had given of themselves so that she could live. Their strength was halved, but the Ones Who Were with them would add their strength to theirs, for that was the Way. She would be guided by the parents of her flesh, mostly by L'nai, until she bore the Touch and knew the merging, for that was the one thing that they could not give her.

"If you grow strong and live," L'nai had taught her, "if the All Father finds you worthy, one day the Call will come and you will seek a fallen one. Then the Ones Who Were will join with you and you will become part of the people. Live and grow strong, D'lia, and you will make us proud."

Deep within her dream, Shelby knew D'lia, the eldest female of the Ones That Were within her, the Great Mother. As she dreamed, the story of D'lia unfolded in a panorama of simplicity and beauty. A story of hardship and survival, of the Rituals and of the Way. She learned of the bounty of the All Father, and she knew the severity of His tests to prove if she was worthy. She learned the nature of the plants and beasts, she grew and flourished, challenged, hunted, killed. She heard the Call and bore the Touch and merged and became part of the people.

As Shelby slept, K'ural, the Great Hunter, most skilled provider of the Ones Who Were with Shelby, kept watch for her. Shelby slept, but the eyes of Shelby's body stayed wide open, staring and questing all about with inhuman alertness. Shelby heard nothing deep within her dream, but every sound that night was audible to her ears, to K'ural, whose body had lived ages ago. And, if the need arose, K'ural could get up and fight or flee to protect the body and the soul while Shelby slept on, unaware.

As D'lia, the Great Mother, gently guided Shelby's dream, K'itar, the elder, the Great Father, plumbed the depths of Shelby's psyche. It was the most dangerous thing K'itar had ever done, but it was necessary. N'tai had been dying in his body, and to save them all he had had no choice but to merge with One Who Was Not. And now they were all within this one, this alien female who had never *been*, yet *was*. Strange and terrifying were the twistings and the turnings of her mind, but K'itar, as eldest, as Great Father, had to find a way for all of them to live within this alien beast that was not a beast. It was a thing of blasphemy and sadness, but it was what was. The Ones Who Were had to survive.

So the Great Father focused all his energies upon this being known as "Shelby Michaels," and he learned that the Shelby creature was, indeed, much more than a beast. Her fellow creatures (of whom she felt afraid!) were known as people too, and they had Rituals and Ways that were all their own, though extremely complex and confusing. And frightening too. K'itar learned that these "humans" did not live as the people lived, were not as pure and simple, but that they did great things. They lived in shelters that were larger than the largest trees, some as big as mountains! They lived together, closer to each other than any of the people would have been able to bear . . . and yet, the Shelby creature could not bear it herself. K'itar learned that the humans also challenged, clashed over domain, but that they fought together, many bodies at one time united in something that they called a "war," and that they used weapons! And the object of a war was not to prove which "side" was stronger by a display of force and skill and bravery, but to prove which was the strongest by the amount of weapons they possessed, by the fearsomeness of their destructive capabilities and by the number of humans that were killed. K'itar recoiled from the horror, but S'tarok, the Healer, gave him strength to continue.

There was so much to learn, so much that seemed mysterious and incomprehensible, that K'itar felt fear and confusion. Yet he could not run away. To guide the body and the soul of Shelby, the One That Is, he needed to understand everything about the sort of being that she was. And he found one thing which gave him hope. He learned that Shelby and the other humans were, indeed, different from the people, very different, but that they were not blasphemous. Strange they were and lonely, but they knew the All Father.

These humans did not worship the All Father in the same way that the people did and they called Him by many names. Some called Him God, some called Him

Buddha, Bog, Jehovah, Allah . . . but there was no mistake, it was the All Father. And it was with wonder that K'itar learned that the All Mother (the Shelby creature called Her by a strange name, "Boomerang") was not alone, but that there were many others like Her! The humans called Them "worlds" and "planets" and They all circled things called "stars," things like the Giver of the Light. To think that there were other beasts and beings living so far away that their "worlds" could not be seen, that the Givers of *their* Light were so far away that they appeared as the dots in the sky at night, that these things were "suns," some of them larger by many times than the Giver of the Light—it amazed K'itar and S'tarok and the others. They knew that it was true, because the Shelby creature had been to those places in something called a "ship," and she had *seen* these things! It filled them with wonder and great reverence, for they had never suspected how great the All Father truly was. Even the humans knew He had created all these things! K'itar and the Ones Who Were became filled with shame, for they had worshiped the All Father for the things He made to grow and for the game He made to run and crawl and fly. They prayed to Him by lying down upon the All Mother to be near Him, never suspecting how far He could reach.

K'itar saw that the All Father had created these humans as a test for the people, that He had made them lonely for a purpose. The humans never heard the Call, they never merged. Their race grew strong as the beasts grew strong, by the survival of the fittest. Few of them knew of the beginnings of their line. There had been Great Fathers before K'itar, Great Mothers before D'lia, and Great Hunters before K'ural. As the ages passed, the merging became much more complete, the stronger becoming much more dominant, absorbing Ones Who Were into themselves so that now K'itar was the Great Father, an amalgam of all those who had gone before, a conglomeration of their strength, their will, their wisdom. But with humans, it was different. Their ancestors left their impression on their minds and bodies, something that the humans called "genetics," but there was no memory, no communion! And to counteract this loneliness, the All Father had invested these humans with great hunger, a drive to always reach beyond the things they knew, the only way they could know wisdom. The All Father had done this so that one day the humans would find the people and the soil, the All Mother within whom the All Father slept. It had been no accident that one of the people had not come in time to answer N'tai's Call. The All Father had made it happen so. All the Ones Who Were saw and understood that they had been chosen for a great and holy task, a true test to see if the people were worthy of the All Father. And the Ones Who Were felt less afraid, for now they all felt honored.

Fannon awoke to the sound of Nils Björnsen softly calling his name. To wake him any other way was to invite injury. He came awake instantly, crawling out of the small shelter they had constructed.

"Trouble?" he asked Nils.

"Nothing I couldn't handle," Nils replied. "We had some visitors a little while ago, don't know what, I just saw the eyes glowing in the dark beyond the fire, but I scared them off. Anyway, it's your watch."

"Right. Should be daylight soon."

"Yes, the sooner the better, even though I wouldn't mind a little extra sleep. At least it hasn't rained."

"Yeah. Well, you can't lose them all."

"You think you'll be able to find the trail again?"

"Ask me in the morning."

"Full of good cheer, aren't you?"

"After nightmares, I usually am. Go to sleep. Excuse me if I don't say pleasant dreams."

Nils entered the lean-to, lay down and was asleep almost instantly. Fannon envied him that ability. He could wake up at once, but going to sleep always presented him with something of a problem. He could never seem to turn off the white noise in his brain.

He sat, cradling the rifle in his lap, wishing that he had a cigarette. In a few hours, it would be daylight. With any luck, a hellhound would wander a bit too close and he'd be able to shoot some breakfast. The meat was surprisingly tasty for such an ugly brute.

For the remaining few hours, his thoughts were about Shelby, who never should have set foot on Boomerang's surface. She was our responsibility, he thought. We should never have left her alone. A pilot would have no chance out in the field. But then this pilot was doing admirably well so far. The training program equipped him with skills necessary for survival in hostile alien environments, but he was very grateful for the things his father had taught him when he was a boy, hunting bison with the old man in Colorado's basement. His father had taught him well. Fannon wondered what Shelby's ancestors were teaching her. He wondered if she could survive the education.

Shelby came awake with the realization that her body had been awake for some time before her. Her mind had needed more rest than her body, and the Shades had understood that. And now that she was awake and fully conscious, Shelby could "remember" what she had been doing while she was asleep.

Once, during the night, K'ural had made her climb a tree to escape a hungry Rhann. Her body was not as good at climbing as that of a Shade, but K'ural had helped her learn. Now she knew she needed to make weapons. Even while she slept, K'ural had found a newly grown sapling, straight and strong, and had uprooted it. Then, using a jagged piece of rock, he had painstakingly stripped off the branches and sharpened its end to a point. The result was the javelin she carried in her left hand. It was not as long as the spears carried by most Shades, for K'ural had taken into consideration her human height and length of arm. Now, she headed for a river that she knew was nearby, although she herself had never seen it.

Shelby knew that while she slept, the Ones Who Were had not been idle. She was now aware of Great Father K'itar and of his efforts to learn everything about her and her kind so that the Ones Who Were could understand and not be frightened, so that a symbiosis could be achieved. And she knew that Great Mother D'lia had been her guide during her dream and she understood what she had been shown. The Ones Who Were no longer frightened her, no longer seemed like alien invaders, but she was not yet completely comfortable with them. They had much to learn about each other, and there was still the question of what she had become. That frightened

Shelby more than anything. Was she now a Shade, one of the people? Or was she still a human . . . only much changed and no longer alone?

Gone entirely was the sleepy, dissociated feeling of the previous day. Shelby felt alive and vibrant. She felt strong, drawing on the strength of the Ones Who Were, and she felt a presence, S'tarok, the Healer, soothing all her uncertainties and fears. She wanted to go back and tell Fannon and Björnsen everything, but she knew that she had to finish making weapons first. She needed a j'par, a nutfruit catapult. For this reason, she was going toward the river. And she felt another need as well, one that she could not entirely define.

Fannon and Björnsen—what would they do? They would most certainly try to follow her and bring her back. And she would have to go back. She could not abandon them. She was their pilot and it was her responsibility to get them back to ColCom safely. Only what would happen then? Could she possibly go on as she had before? Would they let her? How would they react when they discovered, as they would have to, that one of their pilots had merged with alien beings? A large part of her now thought of Boomerang, the All Mother, as her home. It seemed insane, she knew, but it was what was. Could humans ever learn to live with Shades or Shades with humans? She would be the test. The internal conflicts within her were enough to reduce her to a mound of jelly, but the Ones Who Were lent her their strength so that she could carry on.

They were quiescent. She was aware of them, but they did not "speak" to her, even though she knew they could. They didn't really have to, since she could know anything that they knew and vice versa. Speech among the Shades, among the Ones Who Were and One That Is, was more an internal social function and a way to preserve the ancient language. But they didn't speak because they knew she didn't want them to. She wasn't ready yet. They were content to let her try to work things out. But they couldn't quite conceal their anxiety.

She reached the river and laid her javelin down upon the bank. She shucked her clothes and dove into the water, enjoying its delicious coolness. Shelby Michaels did not know how to swim, but the One That Is swam beautifully. She enjoyed the curious phenomenon of swimming like an otter when even in her youth she had been deathly afraid of water. Then she climbed out and found a tree a bit farther down the bank, a tree that extended its roots out from the riverbank and into the water. Guided by K'ural, she held her javelin and looked down into the water, spotted her prey, and her arm seemed to jerk forward of its own volition as she speared a snakelike fish. Before she had a chance to think about it, she found that she had broken off the head and was eating the eel-like creature raw. Shelby's stomach might have turned were it not for the great pleasure which the Ones Who Were felt in devouring the fish. Her existence had become a constant revelation.

Eventually, she found what she was looking for. An appropriately shaped piece of flint—at least it looked like flint—and one of those curious trees that grew down low to the ground, more a bush than a tree, really. Yet this bush had a bole that curved in upon itself, with foliage growing on the inside. As she continued farther down the riverbank, she saw more and more of these growths, and she knew what she was looking for. At a bend in the river, she found a shallow area where the water carved out a piece of the bank and formed a sort of pool, a pocket where the current carried driftwood to the shore. There were several seasoned pieces of driftwood floating there, or resting up against the bank, wood that was once a plant, one of those curved bushes with the strong, treelike bole. She selected one and fished it out of the pool. Then, after having sharpened the piece of flint upon a larger rock, she set about carving the driftwood, stripping off the branches until there was nothing left except the thick, curved wooden bole, worn bare of bark by time spent in the water. Gradually, using the crudely sharpened rock, she fashioned it into a paddle she could comfortably hold, reshaping it somewhat until she had a functional catapult. The result was a curved, cupped paddle about two feet long and about five inches wide, similar in shape and general appearance to the baskets used in the Basque game of jai alai. With this catapult, she would be able to hurl the nutfruit seed pods, which were about the size of

Terran oranges. When these seed pods fell to the ground, they exploded upon impact, and the spores inside were deadly to almost every beast created by the All Father. Deadly to the people too, as well as to humans.

I *am* becoming one of them, she thought. The people *as well as humans.* But the hysteria that might have bubbled forth was quelled by the Great Mother. They were taking care of her. Without them, she would not have survived the night. Might not even have survived the previous day. She was not afraid of them anymore. They could not harm her without harming themselves. And they did not want to harm her. For the first time in her life, it seemed, she had someone to care for her. And there were many of them, generations upon generations, absorbed and intermixed with and into each other. They had no identities as she knew the concept; rather they had dominant aspects. The Great Mother, whom she knew as D'lia, was not an individual, but a manifestation of countless females, a gestalt that she experienced directly. To think of them—her—as D'lia was to think not only of a strong and dominant female, the "leading aspect" of the gestalt, but to think of a microcosm of Shade female history. So it was with the Great Father, K'itar, and with S'tarok, the Healer. With humans, Shelby was but the recent link in the generational chain; with the people, Shelby *was* the generation. And not just one, but many.

The thought of all that knowledge and experience within her was staggering. Only Shelby did not stagger, nor would she. What Shelby Michaels could not cope with, the One That Is, augmented by the Ones Who Were, could handle.

If something like this happened to a computer, Shelby thought, it would no doubt go through the mechanical equivalent of sensory overload. Only in this case, it was the overloading data itself that prevented the breakdown. The insanity that cured itself. And Shelby suddenly realized that one of the results of having merged with the Shades was that she no longer bore the sole responsibility for her welfare and survival. *It was shared.*

For the first time, Shelby began to understand how Wendy must have felt. The Shades—the people—were not telepaths, but they possessed a latent ability, an expanded awareness like a sense, a sixth sense, that if unconsciously projected and picked up by a sensitive like Wendy . . . Small wonder that Wendy had withdrawn. It hurt the Ones Who Were to realize that they had caused harm to an innocent being by wrongly thinking that Wendy was a creature of blasphemy, an evil, cursed thing. They had not done it themselves, but one of the people had, and it was enough to make them feel the burden of guilt.

Whatever happened to her now, Shelby knew that the mission was far from a failure. It was a gloriously unimagined success. ColCom would not receive the answer they wanted to hear. Unquestionably, Boomerang could not be colonized. Yet it was possible that the humans and the people could find a common ground. They had so much to teach each other!

Fannon and Björnsen simply had to know. She had to make them understand the magnitude of what she had discovered, of what she had become. In terms of evolution and technology, certainly, the Shades were not superior to humans. But in terms of psychological strength, emotional makeup, racial memory, experience . . . in so many other ways, they were, if not superior, then infinitely more fortunate. Of course they felt great sadness for the humans! Compared to them, and what they shared together, the human race was to be pitied.

If it were only possible for Shades and humans to interbreed! I was never alive until this day, thought Shelby. I've spent my life hiding from everyone and everything. I found my career inside a womb, and I've lived for years in isolation, afraid, rejected, hurt, unable to stand the company of my fellow human beings. It took an alien race to show me how full life can be. My God, I've never *lived* before!

She dunked her head into the water, trying to clear it. Images and possibilities were whirling around inside her mind; she had not even begun to consider the ramifications of her merging with the people. She tossed back her head and laughed, feeling a wildness welling up within her, an incredible and indescribable energy that filled her with a sense of purpose. She looked up toward the mountains, which had seemed to exert some sort of *pull* on her. She had been wandering in that general direction, not really knowing why. Now, she *knew* why. And it might have terrified Shelby Michaels, but it filled the One That Is with yearning and desire.

Shelby felt the Need.

CHAPTER FIVE

R'yal felt the burning deep inside him as the Ones Who Were guided the body and the soul up the mountain trail, a trail older than time itself. The path that led to it from the forest was well worn. Even the rock beneath his feet bore the traces of countless passages to the mating place of the people, high up in the mountains. It was to be the second mating for the One That Is. Perhaps this time, the All Father would bless the mating with One That Will Be. If they were worthy, it would be so.

It had been a long journey and a hard one. The climb ahead was harder still. The mountains were not without their hazards. But it was the Way. It had been so for generation upon generation. During the time of Need, there was no challenging. One of the people could pass through the domain claimed by another without a test of strength. The Need came to all, and it was a holy thing. It was a time when all the people came together in the place of mating to celebrate the Rituals and the Way. It was the time of choosing, to reaffirm that they were different from the beasts, to celebrate the strength of the All Father and of the Ones That Will Be.

The trail was steep, and R'yal progressed slowly. It was easy to slip and fall, and it was a long, long drop. The path worn into the stone wound around the mountainside like a ledge. There was nothing but the wind between R'yal and the jagged rocks far below. It was the third day of his climb, and he could only travel during the daytime now, when the Giver of the Light could show the way. Though the people could see quite well in the dark, it was too precarious a trail to risk moving at night. One missed step would prove fatal, and the dying would be instantaneous, with no time to give the Call. If R'yal fell, there would be no merging and the One That Is and the Ones Who Were would be no more. So R'yal moved slowly, carefully.

The wind tore at him and tried to pluck him from the ledge. He looked above, to another section of the trail, and he could see one of the people moving on ahead of him. He looked down and he could see more of the people, like tiny specks upon the ground, beginning their climb. The view was spectacular. As far as R'yal could see, the All Mother stretched forth. Far below him, he could see the treetops, like a lush blue-green carpet covering the bosom of the All Mother. He could see the rivers winding through the forests like blue ribbons that reflected light. And, farther away, he could see a brighter reflection, the silvery glow from the monster with no wings in the place where nothing grew. It still waited there, patiently, until the time came when it could learn to stomach the Ones Who Were Not, and then it would doubtless fly away, never to return, the blasphemy removed forever.

R'yal came to the end of the ledge, to an outcropping of rock into which some steps had once been chiseled. Now the steps were little more than worn and smoothed-out hollows in the rock. R'yal picked his way with care, guided by the sureness of the Ones Who Were, who had made this journey many times. A short climb and then another ledge, this one much higher than the first. The wind up here felt stronger. A few hours more and he would reach the place of mating. The urge within him grew stronger by the moment. The strength of the Need made him want to run, to throw all caution to the biting wind, yet he heard constantly the reassurance of N'lia, the Great Mother.

"Go with care, R'yal. You have great strength of will. Your offspring will be strong and one day you too will be a Great Father. Do not fight the Ones Who Were. Be patient, you are almost there. Save your strength for the choosing and the mating. Save your energy for the Rituals."

At the end of this final ledge, there was a chasm. To test his courage, R'yal looked over the edge and down into the abyss. He could not see the bottom. As before, when he had made this journey for the first time in the life of his body and soul, the chasm exerted its inexorable pull. It was yet another test. If the body and the soul were weak, the chasm would win the struggle, would conquer the will and hypnotize it. Then the end would come. None of the people knew how many had succumbed to the pulling of the chasm, to the power of its wind. When first he felt the Need and made the journey, R'yal had seen one of the people fail this test of the All Father. The fall had been long and silent as the body flailed, spinning down into the gorge. It had been an awful sight. R'yal knew that he was strong; he would not fail the test.

He leaned out slightly and looked down into the gaping maw, spitting into its depths to show his contempt for the chasm's hunger. His mane was wild in the wind. The cold winds whirling deep inside the gorge screamed terribly. The chasm seemed to call to him. He imagined he could hear his name being echoed from the depths.

R'yallll . . . R'yalllll . . .

The Ones Who Were supported his will with theirs, and R'yal turned from the gorge, having defeated it. He felt its pull no longer. He had faced it, fought with it, and won.

There remained one final test before the way was clear to the place of mating. The test of sureness. R'yal followed the narrow path around the side of the chasm, hugging the rock wall to lessen the effect of the wind's force upon his body. He slowly edged around the bend, following the chasm's ghastly lip. And then the path switched back, leading back for a short way in the same direction he had come, only this time on the other side of the mass of rock. Then it curved around, still following the chasm's edge, leading to still another flight of steps worn smooth by countless passages. At the top of the steps was the mountain's summit. And leading across the chasm from the summit was a bridge of stone.

Here the winds were fierce indeed. And here it was fatal to look down.

R'yal paused briefly to commune with the Ones Who Were, and together they prayed to the All Father to make the One That Is surefooted. Then, with his head held high, not looking down, R'yal stepped out upon the bridge of stone.

The bridge was thick and strong, he had no fear of its giving way. He only had to fight the winds and his own fear. Even the Ones Who Were could not help him now. This final test was something R'yal had to overcome alone, that was the Way. Yet he felt aware of them and their confidence in the One That Is. And slowly, putting one foot before the other, standing erect and proud, R'yal walked out upon the bridge.

"How many does that make?" asked Fannon.

"I'm not sure. At least two dozen," said Nils.

"Yeah, that's what I figure." Fannon stared up at the trail winding up into the mountains and out of sight. "They're all headed in the same direction," he said, jerking his head at the mountain. "Up there. I wonder why?"

"You're sure she came this way?" said Nils. "You couldn't have made a mistake?"

"She came this way, all right. And she's going to run right into a nest of them. I wonder how they're going to feel about it."

"It doesn't make sense," said Nils. "The Shades don't group together. Where the hell are they all going?"

"You've got me, partner," Fannon said, "but I intend to find that out. We're still on a mission, remember? Besides, that's the way that Shelby went."

"It's crazy. We didn't bring any mountain-climbing gear."

Fannon grinned. "So? Neither did the Shades. Come on, there seems to be a break in traffic. Let's go."

They didn't have any real trouble until the second day. It was on the second day that they passed the treeline. After that, they had to move with extreme care, to avoid being seen by Shades. They had no trouble following the trail, but it was rough going. Nor did they miss the significance of the fact that the trail was obviously centuries old.

They slept in shifts, as they had throughout the journey. Once they passed the treeline, they saw no animals or birds. Everything was solid rock and the mountains appeared to be barren of life. On the third day, they were spotted by two Shades on a level just below them as they were negotiating the ledge. There was nowhere to hide. The first Shade saw them and backed off in surprise. In so doing, it knocked into the one behind it and both went over the edge. It was not a pleasant sight. They made no noise as they fell; there was no screaming.

"Jesus!" whispered Nils. "What a way to go."

"It could happen to us just as easily," said Fannon. "Let's press on. Whatever's at the end of this trail, it must be mighty important for them to risk it."

They *heard* the chasm before they came to it. The wind howling in its depths sounded like the screams of a thousand banshees. And the lip of the ledge that ran around the rock outcropping to a point they could not see where the trail evidently continued was not at all wide. They edged around it, one at a time, not daring to look down. Neither of them wished that they had brought a safety line. They didn't speak of it, but they both knew that the ledge was so precariously narrow that should one of them lose his footing and fall, there was no way that the other would be able to support the weight. Both of them would go. Fannon edged around first, carefully sliding his feet along and feeling his way, back pressed hard against the rock wall behind him. He felt hampered by his pack and rifle, which he had been forced to transfer to his chest, but it was impossible to think of leaving any of the gear behind.

Then Nils started around. His hair and clothing flapped in the wind, his rifle clattered against the rock behind him as it swung from his shoulder. He moved with painstaking slowness, and every time the rifle moved he stopped, not willing to take the chance that even that slight motion might cause him to lose his balance.

"Don't look down," he kept whispering to himself, "don't look down."

Had Shelby made it that far? Or had she . . .

As he was halfway around the bend, he heard Fannon swear. He froze.

"Nils?"

It took a moment for him to find his voice. He stood motionless, eyes closed, afraid that his will would break and that he would look down.

"Ye—" He cleared his throat. "Yes?"

"God, you gave me a fright." Fannon sounded very close, although he still could not see him. "I shouldn't have blurted out like that. For a minute there, I thought you'd gone over the edge."

"Uh . . . no, not yet."

"Funny. Come on, get over here. No, *take your time.*"

Nils needed no urging. He took a deep breath and started sidling sideways once again. Then he was around the bend and there was room to back away from the gorge and catch his breath. He shifted his gear around to his back again, feeling shaky. Fannon was sitting down on the path, leaning against the rock.

"What's the matter? What happened?" Nils asked.

"Take a look," said Fannon, indicating the direction with a short jerk of his head.

Nils looked in the direction Fannon had indicated, and his jaw dropped.

"Holy shit."

It was precisely what Fannon had said moments ago. It had almost made his heart stop then, not knowing what Fannon had run into. Now that he saw it, Nils found that he couldn't swallow. The trail led back a ways, then started to climb again until it curved around the lip of the gorge and ended at a flight of stone steps. The steps led to the crest of the mountain. And across the chasm, on the other side, was a rock wall with what appeared to be a natural cave big enough to drive a crawler through. And between the cave and the summit of the mountain upon which they stood was a mammoth stone span, a natural formation, a bridge. Clearly, it was the way they had to go. *Across that bridge.*

"God, I hate this mission," Fannon said. It was becoming a litany with him.

"There's got to be another way across," said Nils.

Fannon raised his eyebrows. "Who says so?"

"I can't cross that bridge."

"What makes you think *I* can?" asked Fannon. He leaned his head back against the rock.

"The force of wind up there must be tremendous. We'll both be blown right off."

"Aren't you in the least bit curious to see what this is all about? Where this trail leads to?"

"Right this moment, not especially."

"Scared?"

"Absolutely terrified."

"Good."

"Good?"

"Misery loves company. I'd almost rather go back to Rhiannon than cross that bridge. Almost, but not quite."

"It must have been a real horror."

"Yeah. Make you a deal. You make it across that bridge, I'll tell you all about it. All the grisly details."

Nils made a wry face. "That's assuming that *you* make it."

Fannon grinned. "I knew there was something I liked about you, Nils. You always look on the bright side. And you've got a delightful sense of humor. Come on, let's get on with it. If Shelby could make it across that thing, we can."

Nils took a deep breath and let it out slowly. "There's the possibility that she *didn't* make it," he said slowly.

Fannon nodded. "There is that. But it changes nothing. We still have to go. I want to know why the Shades are all flocking up there like a bunch of lemmings."

"Awkwardly put, but concise. You're not afraid of heights, by any chance, are you?"

"Me? Nothing to it."

"Oh. Because, you see, I am."

Fannon stared at him. "You're kidding."

"Actually, I'm not."

"You picked a hell of a fine time to tell me!"

"Seemed like as good a time as any."

"How the hell'd you ever make it through training?"

"I prayed a lot. And when I got back to my quarters, I threw up."

Fannon sighed. "Well, I must say you've hidden it pretty well. You made it this far."

"I never would have made it alone," Nils said.

"You won't be alone up on that bridge, either, partner. I'll be right behind you."

Nils gulped. "You're not going to make me go first?"

"I'm sure as hell not going to let you follow me! That's all I need, you getting halfway across, then freezing. What then?"

"I won't freeze, Drew. I promise. But you mustn't make me go first. I don't think I could stand it."

"You'll stand it, all right."

"Drew, seriously—"

"I'm serious as hell. Nothing doing." He got to his feet and clapped Nils on the shoulder. "Come on, partner, follow the leader. And you're it."

They climbed the trail up to the summit and stood looking out over the chasm. The span looked perilously narrow. Not as narrow as the ledge they had traversed, but there was no rock wall to lean against, no solid reminder of reality except the stone bridge itself. Overbalance either way and . . .

Nils bent from the force of the wind. "Drew, I can barely stand upright. How—"

"You'll crawl."

"But . . . but that means . . . that means I'll be facing down."

"Not necessarily. You can fix your eyes squarely on the other side. Or you can bore right into the rock beneath you and make like an inchworm. I'm in no particular hurry."

"What about my rifle?"

"Sling it over your shoulders and cinch it tight."

"The pack—"

"Push it ahead of you or wear it on your chest and use it as a cushion. Got any more excuses?"

"Suppose some Shades come up behind us?"

"They haven't yet, have they? Except those two we saw before, and they didn't make out so well. I don't think they'll come running out here to shove us off. And if they do, I can shoot lying down."

Nils licked his lips. His throat felt very, very dry. "You'll stay close behind me?"

"If I get any closer, we'll have to get married."

"I'm sorry I'm being such a baby, Drew, it's just that—"

"You can apologize when we get to the other side. Now *move*!"

Nils took a deep breath and got down on all fours. With his rifle slung across his back, he removed his pack and slowly pushed it ahead of him onto the bridge, holding onto one of the straps. Then he followed. He kept his eyes glued to the stone beneath him, his head only inches away from the surface of the bridge. The wind whipped at him. He shoved the pack forward several inches, then slid behind it, bringing his legs up first and then pushing forward, exactly like an inchworm. He didn't dare look up. Push, slide. Push, slide. Push, slide. It didn't seem like much exertion, but within moments he was exhausted. He rested his cheek upon the stone and caught his breath. He had no idea how far across he was. All he heard was the wind howling in his ears.

"Fannon?"

The wind carried his voice away. It had seemed little more than a croak. There was no answer. He screamed.

"Fannon!"

"Whaddya *want*, for God's sake?" Fannon yelled back.

Nils breathed heavily. "Noth—" He raised his voice. "Nothing! I just wanted to be sure you were still there!"

"I'm here, I'm here. Come on, already!"

Nils swallowed and pushed the pack ahead of him. A bit too far too fast. Instead of pushing it gently, straight ahead, he pushed it to the side, toward the sloping edge of the bridge. He felt a sharp tug on the strap and looked up in time to see it go over the edge. Its weight dragged his arm forward suddenly, and in terror he let go. And, in doing so, looked up.

Fannon crawled forward and ran into Björnsen's foot.

"Nils! Keep moving!"

Silence. Björnsen wouldn't budge.

"Nils!"

"Nils!"

"Nils, Goddammit . . ."

Fannon gritted his teeth. They were a little more than halfway across.

"Nils, you son of a bitch, don't you freeze on me!" Fannon yelled hoarsely.

Björnsen hugged the stone as though he were a part of it. If he was blubbering, Fannon couldn't hear it.

"Jesus *Christ* . . ." Fannon inched forward, over Björnsen's foot, and sank his teeth into his calf and bit down hard. It worked. Nils started moving forward once again. Slowly, but he started moving. It seemed like an eternity until they had crossed the bridge, but cross it they did. They entered the cave, leaving the tearing wind behind, and sat down wearily. Fannon leaned back and closed his eyes.

"Congratulations," he said.

"Give me the medpak."

"You had it. It went over the side. Why, you going to be sick?"

"No. I think you drew blood. I was going to take a tetanus shot."

Fannon opened his eyes and looked at Nils. Björnsen smiled weakly.

"Thanks. I'm sorry. I—" And then he was sick.

"Rookie," Fannon muttered. Then he chuckled. Chances were his own pants could stand a laundering.

Shelby followed the guidance of the Ones Who Were, walking confidently through the cavern, which formed a natural tunnel through the rock to a point beyond where light was visible. She felt exhilarated, and the Need was strong within her. When she had first seen the stone bridge across the chasm, she had felt terrified, but her fears had been soothed by the Great Mother and by S'tarok, the Healer. And for the first time, one of them "spoke" within her mind in a language unlike any she had ever heard, but one which she understood.

"This is the final test imposed by the All Father," K'ural the Hunter told her. "To prove their worthiness, the people must cross the span erect and proud and not allow the winds to sway them from their purpose."

She felt the aspect of the Hunter within her as a strong and predatory force, both proud and fierce. The aspect of the Hunter gave her feelings such as she had never felt before, human equivalents of emotions felt by Shades. Shelby had never thought that she would feel strong. She had never suspected that within her was a capacity for confidence, for strength of will, for savage dominance. Yet the presence of the Ones Who Were brought forth within her aspects of her *self* that she had never known, facets of herself that had been repressed and undeveloped because of her own uncertainties and pain, because of fear.

"Shelby"—it felt strange to hear . . . to *feel* . . . the phenomenon of her own mind addressing her by name in such a manner—"within the body and the soul are strengths the One That Is has never used. Within you lies the will to overcome your fears. I am K'ural, Great Hunter, the sum"—K'ural used the English word "sum," which startled her—"of many great and noble hunters. The One That Is, though not truly of the people, knows the will of the All Father. The One That Is has merged with the Ones Who Were. Within you now is the skill and courage of the Great Hunter. The Great Hunter has crossed the span many, many times. The body and the soul have never crossed this bridge. Yet the One That Is can remember having crossed it."

Shelby *could* remember. Physically, she had never crossed the bridge of stone herself, of course, which was what K'ural had meant when he said that the "body and the soul" had never crossed it. But she had the memories of many, many crossings. She experienced those memories, and as she did, T'lan "spoke" within her.

"I am T'lan, Father Who Walked in Shadow," he said.

She felt T'lan within her in a way that would have petrified her if not for the presence of N'lia and S'tarok. T'lan slithered across her consciousness like a reptile. There was the sense of incredible power and bestial rage, of something which, in human terms, could only be described as Evil, only human terms did not apply.

"Among the people, there are those who walk in shadow, there is strength that derives from a closeness to the beasts and from bonds to ancient things, things that were *not* people, but things from which the people sprang. The Great Hunter has the skill to stalk and kill, yet it is the Father Who Walked in Shadow who provides the spirit and the instinct. Within the One That Is, that spirit sleeps. T'lan shall awaken it and the body and the soul will cross the bridge."

Shelby remembered all the crossings and knew that it

could be done. The Ones Who Were would do it for her. She gauged the wind and walked out upon the span. She didn't hesitate . . . *they* didn't hesitate. The wind shifted and almost threw her off, but Shelby fought for balance, leaned against the wind, but braced in such a manner that if it quit suddenly, she would not topple. She did not look down, but kept her eyes focused on her goal, the cavern mouth on the other side. And she crossed the bridge, erect. She entered the cavern and looked back, astounded that Shelby's body had accomplished something that Shelby would never have been able to do.

"Shelby did it," said K'itar, the Great Father.

"The One That Is must cross the bridge alone," N'lia told her. "That is the Way. The Ones Who Were can help the spirit just before the crossing, they can prepare the body and the soul, but they cannot guide the crossing. That the One That Is must do alone. Shelby may not be of the people, but Shelby has proved worthy."

Within her, Shelby heard a wild sound, a cry that she knew was the way the people laughed. She felt the Great Hunter's mirth and laughed with him. T'lan did not respond, but he had done his work. Something deep inside her had, indeed, awakened.

R'yal stepped forth into the light. He was filled with expectation. Before him stretched forth a box canyon, surrounded on all sides by sheer walls of stone. Far below him, in the center of the canyon floor, bubbled the Spring of Life, sending clouds of steam into the mating place and giving it warmth.

He could see the people preparing for the Rituals. There were many of them, very many, and that meant many females for the choosing. R'yal's breathing quickened, and he wished that one of those females was within reach at that very moment, but then he remembered that that was the Way of the beasts, and he fought to master his impatience. The Need was great and the Need was holy. It had to be acknowledged, but it could not be allowed to dominate the soul.

Walking slowly, summoning up the will to control his trembling muscles, R'yal started down the trail that led to the canyon floor. The Ones Who Were within him shared in his excitement. It took a long time to reach the canyon floor, and by the time he did, he could feel the contagious sexual excitement of the people present. He could feel the heat from the Spring of Life.

It was the only time when the people came together in one place, but there was still a separation. The males and females stayed in separate groups; otherwise the physical proximity would prove too strong a temptation. R'yal could see the females gathering together at one side of the canyon, and he felt an almost uncontrollable lust. His sex organ, no longer retracted, was erect and on display, engorged with his blood and showing all the other males his virility. He strutted proudly into their midst, seeing that some of the older males, having passed their sexual prime without their seed having been blessed, looked upon him enviously. Soon they would be too old to feel the Need and it would not come to them. They would never know the joy of having fathered One That Will Be. R'yal felt sorry for them. With so many virile young males present, the older ones would do poorly in the choosing, and chances were that they would not get the chance to mate with a female. The pain of sexual frustration was intense and pitiful. R'yal had only seen one time of Need before, and an offspring had not been born. His seed had not been blessed. He hoped that this time he would prove worthy. He did not want to be like the older males, who would be passed by in favor of younger and stronger ones. The best that the older males could hope for was a female past her prime. Females still felt the Need at a time when a male of the same physical age had passed beyond it. Many of the older females were very beautiful, but R'yal wanted a young one.

When the Giver's Sentinel passed over the canyon for the second time, the Rituals would begin. It was already dark, and all eyes were turned skyward. Soon the Sentinel would make the first passage and the preparations would begin.

He could tell that the females were anxious. They were milling about and there seemed to be a great deal of activity in their midst. More so than he had remembered from the last time.

"There is an unease over there," N'lia said within him. "The females seem to be restless and disturbed."

"They await the preparation for the Rituals," said R'yal.

"No, R'yal," the Great Mother replied. "The Ones Who Were have seen a great many times of Need, many, many matings. This time, there is something different. Something is disturbing the females."

"There is a strangeness," H'lai Who Walked in Shadow said. "I can sense it."

"Danger?" said T'ran. "How can there be danger in the place of mating?"

"Not danger," said H'lai. R'yal felt tense from H'lai's questing, searching for the feelings that would alert them all to what was happening where the females waited.

"What then?"

"I do not know. But it would be well to stay alert. Something is wrong."

Shelby looked up as the moon passed over the canyon. There was quite a large group of females around her, encircling her, but they made no move toward her. They did not seem to know just what to do. She could imagine how they felt. An alien being had somehow penetrated into their most sacred place, a being who did not belong. And yet, in spite of appearances, she knew that she felt right to them. And they were confused.

It was just like that female she had met the first time she went out after having felt the Touch. Had the Shades not been so intelligent, she might have been killed. But they did not know how to react. It was as if a human family suddenly had an unexpected guest for dinner, a gorilla, but the gorilla *acted* human. It knew all the customs, it could use a knife and fork and take part in the dinner conversation. It would have seemed funny had not Shelby felt so nervous and afraid. The effect she had upon the Shades was electric. None of them came close to her, but as many as could gathered around, staring, starting to venture closer and then pulling back.

"Do not feel afraid," D'lia told her. "The people do not yet understand. They can sense the Ones Who Were within you, but you seem incomprehensible to them. They do not know that you are a test sent from the All Father."

Well, perhaps she was. Shelby had never been especially religious, but she had been raised as a Catholic and certain imprintations always remained, despite the doubts. She had no answers. What were the chances of traveling light-years away from Earth, only to find a sentient, humanoid race that believed in God? They thought it was the same God she had worshiped as a child. Our Father, All Father . . . who was she to say it wasn't? If she ever got back to Earth, the theologists would have a field day with her. As would the scientists at ColCom, the news media, the politicians. . . . Earth, Terra, no matter what one called it, there was still a name that did not apply for her and that was home.

Yet how could Boomerang be home? How could she survive, living in the forest like an animal? How could she reconcile herself to a simple, natural existence? To hunt, to forage, to live close to the land, worshiping it—was that what lay ahead for her? Never again to pilot a ship, never to know the splendid isolation of deep space. Could she leave all that behind?

The Shades were not her kind, but then she had left her kind behind when she had enlisted in the service and become a pilot. She felt a greater degree of intimacy with the Shades within her than she'd ever felt with another human being. If she stopped to think about it, she grew terrified, but the Ones Who Were would not allow her to dwell upon what had happened to her . . . and to them. They needed to survive, and they sensed that she was on the edge. The balance was continually shifting. At times she was dominant, and at other times the Shades were strong within her. She knew that they respected her strength. They had never come up against the concept of an individual identity. To them, life consisted of a sharing, of a gestalt, of a unity with the present and the past. D'lia did not think of herself as an individual, at least not in the way that a human would. She did not understand the concept of a loss of identity. She had nothing to relate it to.

Yet the gestalt within her perceived on an intuitive level that it was important for Shelby to stay in touch with Shelby, with her own uniqueness. They saw this as a sad thing, and it frightened them. She was aware of their feeling of rejection. In cases of pronounced schizophrenia, of split personalities, there was often a battle for control. There was nothing like that with the Ones Who Were. Rather, there was a battle for coexistence.

When she tried to reason it all out, she tried to overpower the sense of them within her. They lacked the sophistication of humans, they had not evolved as far or in the same manner, so in many ways, her will was stronger. But the strength of her own will was a handicap to her finding a way to deal with what had happened to her, because as she fought to maintain control, she frightened them and they withdrew. Then the full significance of her plight blazed forth to bring her to the brink of hysteria, at which point her will crumbled and the Ones Who Were would lend her strength and soothe her, and even though they didn't fully understand, they would bring her back from the edge of insanity. And what was her sanity except her sense of her own reality? To most humans, pilots were not sane. She did not think of herself as being mad, but her present reality was an insane reality, so what *was* there for her to hold onto? And, to make things worse, there was the Need.

She understood it now, but there was nothing she could do about it. It was madness, this uncontrollable urge to couple with an alien being, but at the same time it filled her with a sense of wild abandon and exhilaration. Like a battering ram, it had breached her gates, the defenses she had carefully constructed over the years, allowing the full strength of her loneliness and sexuality to burst forth. She *wanted* to feel a penis inside her, she longed to experience an orgasm and to feel the heat of a male's ejaculation. She felt incredibly turned on; she was terrified but the fear only served to excite her further. The Shades were built very similarly to humans. She saw the erect penis of a male as he passed her, hidden behind a rock on the trail that led into the canyon. He had not seen her, but the sight of him had been enough to lubricate her. Could those possibly be *her* feelings?

She was a woman, not a bitch in heat. Or was she? The Shades within her *were* in heat and she *felt* it. It was a part of her; how could it be denied? She had no doubt that she could accommodate a Shade male. Their organs were different from those of human males in that they were more muscular and could be retracted. The penis of the male who had passed her on the path that led into the canyon was thin and somewhat shorter than that of the only man she had ever slept with, but all she knew was what she saw. It could be dangerous. And could she be impregnated by a Shade? And, if she could, what would she give birth to? If she were to become pregnant . . .

It made her insides churn, but at the same time, she wanted it. She wanted to have One That Will Be growing inside her. If only she didn't feel the Need so strongly, if only she were capable of making a rational decision . . . but there was nothing rational about merging with an alien race. It seemed to Shelby that her fate had been thrown to the winds. She could not fight it. And it frightened her to realize that, deep down inside, she didn't really want to. The Shades were beautiful. She had seen that even before the merging. They were lovely to look at. And now she was responding to them as a Shade, a female in heat.

"The All Father is infinitely wise," K'itar, the Great Father, said, knowing full well her anguish. "You were chosen for a reason. It is not for us to question the All Father. The One That Is has a memory of mating with one of her own kind. It was not a sacred thing. The memory is one of pain. I do not fully understand this memory, but the people do not mate in such a manner. To the people, mating is a reaffirmation of life. It is a hunger, but it is not a hunger to appease the body alone, but the spirit and the soul, as well. Your kind does not feel the Need as we do. I perceive that it is possible for a human to feel the Need at any time. I perceive that humans also have their Rituals, but they are not like ours. The people do not deceive"—he used the English word, there being no Shade equivalent. "They do not manipulate so that they can only take and give nothing in return. It is a Need to reaffirm the joy of life. Not all matings are blessed by the All Father. But even if there is no blessing, even if One That Will Be does not begin to grow within you, there is still the joy of mating. And, for the Ones Who Were, it brings forth the joys of all the births that have gone before. It is the Way and it is what makes the people different from the beasts. What I perceive of your one and only memory of mating tells me that this human male was much like a beast. Perhaps all human males are so. We are different. We are not like beasts. There will be no pain."

CHAPTER SIX

Fannon and Björnsen nestled in the rocks in a small hollow above the trail that led down into the canyon. It was dark, but both men could see quite well through the detachable infrared scopes they had mounted on their rifles. They sat, aiming their weapons down into the canyon, looking for any sign of Shelby.

"You see her?" Fannon asked.

"Not yet," said Nils.

"You think she's down there?"

"If she didn't have an accident getting here, she's down there somewhere."

"You don't think the Shades would harm her, do you?"

"I don't think so, but then I didn't think they grouped together like this, either. Must be thousands of them down there."

They had been sitting there for several hours, watching, waiting, trying to decide upon a course of action. Neither of the two men wanted to venture any closer until they had at least some indication of what was going on down in the canyon. They had seen that the Shades were gathered into two large groups on opposite sides, in the dark. In the center of the canyon was what appeared to be some sort of volcanic pool, casting a surreal light for some distance around the center. The Shades were mostly in the darkness. And their view was obscured in part by the rocks where they hid, so it was possible that Shelby was down there, but not where they could see her. If, indeed, they could pick her out among the throng. The magnification on their scopes enabled them to see fairly closely, but it was still like looking for a needle in a haystack.

The moon passed over the canyon for the second time and the two groups of Shades began to move closer together, toward the area lit by the steaming pool.

"Damn, I wish we'd brought a camera," said Nils.

"You know what this sorta reminds me of?" said Fannon. "A very old film called *King Kong*."

"I don't know it."

"Just as well, because we're going to have to get down there."

Cautiously, they started down the trail. They did not encounter any Shades along the way. They moved slowly down, watching the activity below them. It was all eerily silent, like a fantastic dream. There was no sound except the wind whistling through the canyon. And, as they descended further, they felt some of the heat from the volcanic pool. The temperature down on the canyon floor had to be intense.

"What do you think it is?" asked Nils. "Some sort of tribal ritual?"

"I don't know," said Fannon. "I still don't think they have tribes." Thinking about what it might or might not be was unnerving him. Nothing about this mission had proved predictable. He raised his weapon to take another look through the scope. And swore.

"What is it?" Nils asked, stopping and looking at Fannon with alarm.

"Take a look," said Fannon. "Look at the male Shades."

"I don't see what—"

"Look lower."

"Good God. They're all . . ."

"At attention, every one of 'em. Guess what, partner? I think we're about to find out how they mate."

"But Shelby's down there!"

"Maybe. She—"

"No, I can *see* her!"

"Where?"

"Use the pool as center, follow along from there at ten o'clock."

Fannon swung his rifle, searching. "I can't see her."

"Here, look, line it up with mine."

He moved over to stand by Björnsen and aimed his rifle in the same direction. A moment later, he had her spotted. She was like an island in a sea of Shades. And all the Shades around her seemed to be females. It was hard to tell, the way they kept moving about. There was a kinetic energy about them, a restlessness. . . .

She had stripped off her clothing. Under maximum magnification, Fannon could see that she was perspiring heavily. The sweat made her skin glow in the flickering light. She appeared to be in some sort of trance. And none of the Shades around her would go near her. But they knew she was there, all right. Like a specter at the wedding.

"Shit! Let's haul ass down there," Fannon said. "Any of 'em get in the way, shoot!"

It felt as if she were removed from what was happening. The Ones Who Were had taken over, guiding her along. It was the Ritual of Preparation. It was the time to establish the pattern for the mating. The younger, stronger females and males would be first to take part in the choosing, as it would be the first mating for many of them and they had the best chances of giving birth to strong offspring. The females mingled among themselves, the older ones moving toward the rear, away from the Spring of Life, the younger going forward, within sight of the males. The males would be doing the same thing. It was all accomplished without any communication, but there was a wildness among the females that was not born of the Need. It was her, of course. They all drew back from her as though she were diseased, and the feeling spread throughout them all. She was like a bear come down out of the mountains into a corral full of horses. They were frightened and confused, jostling each other in an effort to stay away from her.

Part of her wanted to run, to escape the insane spectacle, and part of her urged her onward, forward, toward the males. She wound up in front, as though the crowd of females had vomited her out, spitting her out and away from them. And then the males saw her. And all activity stopped.

It spread like a ripple that turned into a wave. As they all became aware of her, all motion ceased. There was only the hissing and the bubbling of the Spring of Life and the sound of wind whistling through the canyon. If not for the strength of the wind, the heat would have been unbearable. It was almost more than she could take as it was. She saw the males through the dancing heat waves and she wanted to flee.

"I can't," she said. "Oh, God, no, I *can't* . . ." But she moved forward.

Several other females, feeling the Need stronger than they felt their fear of her, moved forward with her, and they began to dance, Shelby along with them. Her body seemed to move of its own accord as she watched herself from somewhere outside. She felt D'lia guiding her, enraptured by the Need.

It was a dance like nothing she had seen or heard of. The females moved sinuously, showing off their youth and strength. Their muscles rippled in the glow from the Spring of Life, their bodies gleamed with sweat. Shelby could smell the overpowering scent of them, and she abandoned all her fears. She gave up struggling with D'lia for control, although it had been a halfhearted struggle at best. She felt it, too.

They leaped about, displaying their agility and grace; they moved in pantomimes of challenge, showing how they could win and hold their domains; they made hurling motions with their j'pars and they killed imaginary beasts with their javelins, stabbing hellhounds and twisting the points of the spears in imaginary entrails. Shelby lost herself in the spirit of the dance, in the sheer joy of it. She displayed herself along with the Shade females, throwing in a few improvisations of her own. They all undulated, reveling in their sexuality, thrusting with their hips, swaying with their legs apart, feeling the full force of the Need.

Then some of the males moved forward to join them. There was no attempt at pairing off. Rather, the males also danced by themselves, making the same motions as the females, letting the spirit take them and dancing with a frenzy born of the infectious fever they sensed in one another. Behind the dancers, the waiting groups of males and females swayed together, awaiting their turn for the choosing. For it had now begun.

The males now danced in one place, where they stood, while the females danced around them, circling them, each choosing the one she wanted. Shelby found herself moving toward a male who danced near her, one who could not seem to tear his eyes away from her.

They had all forgotten about her now, their fear and confusion gone in the frenzy of the Need. All around her, females made their choice as they leaped upon males and bore them down. This one, she thought, breathing heavily as she danced around and in front of the astonished male. This one is ours. This one is *mine.*

R'yal's eyes were riveted to the female who danced before him. *One Who Was Not!* How had she come to the place of mating? How had she passed the tests of the All Father? Yet R'yal sensed the Ones Who Were within her, and he realized that they were guiding her. Were guiding her!

"R'yal!" he heard T'ran admonish him. *"R'yal, move away! This cannot be! It is a blasphemy! She is One Who Was Not!"*

But she did not feel like One Who Was Not. And she looked less like One Who Was Not than she had before. It seemed that she had somehow shed the strange skin that she wore when R'yal had seen her last, and now she looked more like one of the people. And she looked different, too. She looked stronger, she leaped higher, and there was a fascination about the way she moved.

R'yal was strong. He was the One That Is. The One That Is knew that the time would come when he would be a Great Father or a Great Hunter. He had never lost a challenge. His game had never escaped him. He longed to guide this mating and he found himself fighting the Ones Who Were, resisting the guiding of T'ran. The Need was very strong within him and he felt an incredible desire for this alien female. She was different. None of the others were like her at all. There was an almost bestial savagery about her, an incredible sense of power in the way she moved and looked at him. He wanted her to choose him. He wanted to put his seed inside her, blasphemy or not.

The Need was felt by the Ones Who Were within him too, and the frenzy of the Need weakened their collective will. R'yal forced T'ran and the others away, forced them away until *he* was guiding, the One That Is, *he* was dancing, showing this strange female his strength and grace. Showing her how he had won his domain and how he slayed the beasts. The desire within R'yal was overpowering as she came up close to him, swaying from side to side. He waited for her to leap upon him, but she did not. For a moment, he thought she would not choose him, but then she did an amazing thing. She stopped dancing and put her hands upon his shoulders, moved her face toward him and placed her mouth over his. She hugged him close to her and he felt her tongue slide between his lips. The Ones Who Were within him recoiled from the contact, but R'yal did not, could not. He felt her tongue moving against his, and it felt strange. Experimentally, he moved his own tongue. What could it mean? Was this some new Ritual he did not know about? Then, abruptly, she removed her mouth from his and, as he stood stock still, astounded, he felt her tongue and lips moving down the wet length of his body, her hands touching him everywhere. With terror, he realized that she was about to take his organ in her mouth! For one agonizing moment, he thought this alien female or beast would try to consume him, but then he felt her mouth upon him and she did not bite or tear, but instead sucked from him, as if she could draw his seed forth like water from a pool. He recalled his feelings during his first mating, that indescribable joy and wonderful sensation, and he felt it now, only differently. R'yal moved his hands down upon her head, forcing himself farther inside her, thrusting deeply, abandoning himself to this wild new sensation. Then suddenly he felt T'ran and D'val strong within him and he realized what they meant to do. And, before he could stop them, they Touched the alien female.

And she screamed.

Shelby's scream cut through the frenzied silence like a razor. The dancers froze in midmotion; even the Shades coupling upon the canyon floor were shocked into immobility at the sound. And it was at that moment that Fannon and Björnsen smashed their way between the two groups of Shades that surrounded the mating couples. Shades were sent sprawling as the two men plowed through them like juggernauts. Fannon, taking in the scene instantly, raised his rifle and shot R'yal. The Shade fell to the ground, not dead, but stunned into unconsciousness.

Shelby writhed upon the ground, in agony. Nils rushed to her while Fannon swung the weapon about, picked out a Shade at random and fired again. Then a third time, quickly. The press began as the Shades flowed back away from them like a receding tide. Fannon felt like killing. He almost hoped they'd force him to.

"Nils! Grab her and let's get the hell out of here before they figure out what's going on!"

"I can't, she's thrashing all about, she . . . I can't hold onto her!"

There was panic in Björnsen's voice. Fannon could not afford to have Björnsen panic. They still had to get down the mountain. He moved quickly to stand over Nils and Shelby, glanced down, shifted his rifle so that its bore was pointing down, and, with a grimace, he fired a stun charge into her. She went limp.

"Drew, for God's sake—"

"Snap to, Nils. Cover me or we're dead. For all they know, we just killed their friends."

Nils held his rifle up, pointing it at the Shades. Several of the males moved forward, and Nils hesitated, then dropped them. Fannon, the stronger of the two, picked Shelby up and threw her over his shoulder in a fireman's carry. Then he took off at a dead run.

He never looked back, trusting to Nils for protection. He needed all his energy to carry Shelby back up the trail. They still had a long way to go, and she was heavy. Fannon was in phenomenal physical condition, and he thanked his lucky stars that he had spent so much time working on his body. Soon he was breathing heavily, laboring to put one foot in front of the other. He pushed himself, blanking out the pain, concentrating only on the effort it took to keep on moving. He could no longer run, or even walk quickly. If the Shades were behind them, they would be able to catch up easily, but fortunately the path was narrow and Nils had the range on them easily. About a third of the way up the trail, he had to stop.

"Nils . . . take her . . . I can't . . ."

"It's all right," he heard Björnsen say. "They're not following."

Fannon let Shelby down onto the ground.

"You sure?"

"Positive. They're buzzing about down there like bees in a hive, but they're not coming after us." Nils sighted through his scope. "The ones we stunned seem to be getting all the attention."

"Well . . . let's hope they . . . don't . . ." Fannon fought to catch his breath. ". . . have a short . . . attention span. C'mon."

Nils handed him his rifle back and his own as well, then he took up the burden. Fannon hung back, keeping a constant watch on the activity of the Shades. He hoped that they wouldn't get unlucky and run into any latecomers heading down the trail. Nils had his hands full carrying Shelby. After what seemed like an eternity, they were at the entrance to the natural tunnel that led to the stone bridge. They plunged inside and staggered through. When they came close to the opposite end, with the stone bridge just beyond, they stopped. Both men sank down to the ground, although they kept their weapons ready. They were exhausted. They had taken several turns each carrying Shelby, who was starting to come around. They needed desperately to rest, and there was no question about crossing the bridge until daylight. To try doing it in the dark, even fully rested, would be suicide. Fannon still had Björnsen's fear of heights to contend with. And Shelby.

"What now?" asked Nils, breathing heavily. His voice echoed in the cavern.

"We wait till morning. And hope like hell the Shades don't come after us."

"Suppose they do?"

"Then we're in a lot of trouble."

"Hey," said Nils, "remember you promised to tell me about Rhiannon?"

"Yeah?"

"Well, I don't want to hear about it."

"Think I know what you mean." Shelby moaned and stirred. "Think we might have a problem."

"Just one?"

"It occurs to me that she might not want to get across that bridge. And there's no way we can force her."

"Try biting her leg off."

Fannon chuckled. "You know, you're really something, partner. Don't take this wrong, but I would've given my right arm to have had you with me on Rhiannon."

Nils looked up at him and smiled. "Thanks."

"You ever thought about retirement?" asked Fannon.

Nils did not respond at once. "A few times."

"Well, if we make it out of here in one piece, what do you say to going halves on a nice little spacer bar somewhere?"

"It wasn't exactly what I had in mind," said Nils, "but it sounds rather nice."

"What did you have in mind?"

Nils shrugged. "It doesn't really matter, does it?"

Fannon sighed. "No, guess not."

Shelby groaned and tried to sit up. Nils helped her. She looked at him blankly for a moment.

"Nils . . ."

"Are you all right?" he asked.

She rubbed her forehead and made a sort of nod, not really definite. She swallowed and licked her lips. "Dizzy," she said.

"You might have a concussion."

"Shit, I hope not," Fannon said.

She looked at him and her eyes seemed empty.

"They're gone," she said.

"So far, they haven't come looking for us," Fannon replied, misunderstanding. "We had to stun several of them. Maybe we scared them off."

She shook her head. "No. They're gone." She leaned her head back against the stone. "Took them away," she mumbled, then fell instantly asleep.

The two men let Shelby have her rest while they took turns keeping watch. Neither of them slept. They felt too edgy to do more than simply lie down and try to relax as best they could. The Shades had still not followed them.

Perhaps they wouldn't, but they wanted to take no chances. They talked idly, quietly, but as the night wore on, they ran out of things to say. The situation was too strained. Both of them kept thinking about the stone bridge. Shelby slept deeply.

At first light, they gathered up their packs and gently woke Shelby. She complained of a headache, but other than that, said nothing. They didn't press her. Instead they looked at each other grimly and, with Shelby walking between them, went out to the bridge.

"One of us is going to have to cross first, to cover the others from the opposite side," said Fannon. This was what he had been afraid of. He didn't want to trust Nils to help Shelby. And he didn't think she'd make it on her own.

"I'll do it," Shelby said flatly.

Nils shook his head. She didn't wait for him to finish. Instead, she took Fannon's rifle and walked out upon the bridge. The two men stared at her in astonishment.

She stood erect, slightly pigeon-toed, using body English to compensate for the force of the wind. She swayed slightly, moving slowly but without hesitation. It looked as though she would fall at any moment. But she didn't fall.

"I see it," Fannon said softly, "but I don't believe it."

Nils swallowed hard. "Well, I *know* I can't walk across like that, but if she can walk it, I sure as hell can crawl."

Shelby made it to the opposite side and stood ready with Fannon's rifle. A short while later, both men had crawled across. Nils had kept his eyes glued to the rock surface immediately before him as he crawled. Nothing would have induced him to look up . . . or down. He set his teeth and inched his way across in wormlike fashion, and only the appearance of Shelby's feet in front of him alerted him to the fact that he had made it.

The rest of that first day saw the most difficult part of the descent. And Shelby led the way. In the face of his own fear, Nils worried about Shelby's seeming lack of it. It wasn't that his ego was on the line—he knew his shortcomings—but she took chances. She wasn't careless, but it made no sense to take the risks she took. Unless she wanted to. . . . Nils didn't want to think about the *unless*. In many ways, she seemed to have changed, but in other ways, she seemed like the old Shelby. And it wasn't until they camped for the second night, almost down the mountain, that she broke her self-imposed silence.

"I need some roots from those plants with the prong-shaped leaves," she said wearily.

"What?" asked Fannon. "Why?"

It took an effort for her to talk. "To chew on. They have healing properties when mashed up and applied to the skin."

They didn't ask how she knew, but for the first time they noticed that she had taken a lot of punishment. Her feet were badly cut up by the rocks, and she was scratched and bruised all over. She huddled by the small fire they had made behind some rocks, shivering. They were now into the foothills and it was considerably warmer, and the trees cut down the wind to almost nothing, but still she shivered.

Fannon cursed himself and removed his shirt to drape around her.

"Would you believe I forgot she was naked?" he said to Nils.

She smiled. "Thanks for the compliment."

"How do you feel?"

She stared into the flames.

"Drained." There was a vacant look upon her face. "That's what they did to me, they drained me. They took them all away."

"I don't understand," said Nils.

"The Shades inside me, the people," she replied. "All gone. I was never meant to have them, so they took them back."

Fannon hesitated. "Is that all they took?"

She shrugged. "I'm just plain Shelby Michaels once again, ship's pilot. I may not be the same anymore, but I'm back to normal. Whatever that means."

"Thank God," said Nils.

Fannon picked up his rifle and rose to his feet. "I'll see what I can do to find some of those roots for you. We lost our medpak, so we're going to have to do the best we can with whatever it is you've learned, at least until we return to the lighter."

He didn't hear what Shelby murmured as he left, but Nils did, and it worried him.

She said, "I miss them."

R'yal moved slowly down the trail, still feeling shaky from what the aliens had done to him. The Ones Who Were within him had to guide him across the bridge, and even they felt the shock of the weapons of the Ones Who Were Not. Yet there was an understanding of those weapons. They could kill, but they could also stun. And the Ones Who Were Not had chosen not to kill.

The union of the Ones Who Were within the alien female and the Ones Who Were within R'yal had produced an understanding of the strange new beings. T'ran had merged with K'itar, and they now knew the terrible mistake that had been made. And it was not the aliens who were blasphemous, but themselves, for they had gone against the will of the All Father. The All Father had decreed that the alien female merge with the people. And they had taken the people away from her, dooming her once again to the loneliness and despair of her kind. It was a burden and a guilt that the Ones Who Were could not bear. They would have to guide the One That Is to find the lonely beings and somehow set things right.

The Ones Who Were within R'yal felt afraid, for none of them had ever Touched a still-living person. The Touch was to be bestowed only at the moment of dying. Yet in their outrage at what they perceived to be a blasphemy in the face of the All Father, the Ones Who Were within R'yal had Touched Shelby and there had been a merging. And they had taken back the people. Yet the strength of the Touch had taken more than they had meant to take. The Ones Who Were within the alien female had been drawn into R'yal, but a part of Shelby had come with them.

That part was not theirs to keep, but it could not be returned without great harm to the One That Is.

The Ones Who Were knew that the strange new beings were very wise in many ways that they did not understand. Perhaps, with their wonderful tools, they would be able to find a way to restore the missing part of Shelby to herself. They did not know how this could be done or why, if they could do it, the aliens had never found a way to merge themselves, but they knew that the way the aliens went was the way they had to go. The All Father had imposed upon them a stern test. And they had failed.

The part of Shelby they had taken inadvertently was a frightened thing. It cowered in their midst, trying to hide from them, trying desperately to keep them at bay. But it could not. It had no strength, no will. It was among them like a wounded animal, and its terror was a pitiful thing. They knew Shelby through this part of her, and they knew the pain she had gone through before and the pain that they had caused her.

For once, all the wisdom of the Ones Who Were could not guide them to seek a solution to their plight. Confused, frightened and guilt-ridden, R'yal started down the mountain, following the Ones Who Were Not. The gestalt that was R'yal did not know what would happen on the road ahead, but there was no turning back. R'yal had become an outcast. With the fever of the Need departed, the people recalled his communion with One Who Was Not, and now they sensed that which was Shelby within him. R'yal had been shunned. The Ones Who Were within him had acted, and now they had to bear the punishment. It was the will of the All Father and it was the Way.

CHAPTER SEVEN

The old distance was between them once again. Nils sat by the fire, keeping watch, his rifle cradled in his lap. Fannon slept while Shelby rubbed the root balm into the soles of her feet. The flickering firelight gave a surreal tint to her features as she sat there on the ground, seemingly absorbed in the task of tending to her injuries. She looked like some sort of aborigine, dressed only in the shirts of the two men. She wore Nils' shirt unbuttoned about halfway down, and Fannon's considerably larger shirt she wore as a makeshift skirt, the sleeves knotted around her waist. Fannon had shot a pair of shoes for her. Under the circumstances, the best that they had been able to do was to skin a hellhound that had wandered a bit too close to their camp. She now had two large pieces of hide, which she could wrap around her feet like crude leggings, holding them in place with hemp. They didn't smell nice, but at least her feet would not get cut anymore.

Nils could not look at her feet without wincing. They were a mess. She should have been in a great deal of pain, but she showed no signs of feeling anything except exhaustion. It was as though her sensory nerves had all been severed. She *should* have been in pain. The way her feet looked, she should have been barely able to walk.

She looked up and met his gaze, and after a moment Nils had to look away. He couldn't meet that feral stare. It was like looking into the eyes of a starving animal.

There was something terribly wrong with her, but he had no way of knowing what it was or what to do about it. No human being had ever experienced what she had been through. There was no telling what effect it had had upon her. Her sanity, whatever was left of it, could be hanging by a thread. But then, pilots weren't supposed to be sane, were they?

How could she not feel the pain? There were a thousand things that could be wrong with her. Perhaps the mind jolt she had experienced had somehow damaged her. There were diseases, such as syringomyelia, which attacked the nerve fibers in the spinal column, which could cause the victim to lose the ability to feel pain. On an alien world, there was no way of knowing what sort of diseases she could contract, what sort of infections might have set in. Until they got her back to the ship, there wasn't even anything that he could do about her injuries short of watching her rub the root balm into her wounds. He didn't like it, he knew nothing about the pulp she was smearing herself with, but she seemed sure of what she was doing and it seemed to comfort her. Nils cursed himself for the fear which had caused him to drop the pack containing their medical supplies.

He envied Fannon for being able to sleep. Their situation had reversed. Fannon, who was plagued by nightmares, fell asleep almost instantly. He had worked the hardest, getting them down that mountain trail. His exhaustion was greater than his nervous strain. Or perhaps it wasn't. Perhaps his mind sought refuge in the oblivion of sleep. He wasn't dreaming, his eyes were still. No. Even as he watched him, Fannon entered his REM cycle and groaned in his sleep. His head moved from side to side as he fought the nightmare. Nils almost spoke to him, but then he did not. Nightmare or not, Fannon needed his rest. They were still at least a day away from their lighter. And it was almost dawn.

With a start, Fannon woke, sitting bolt upright. Nils flinched, startled. Fannon sighed heavily.

"Shit," he said quietly.

"A bad one?"

"Yeah. Don't even ask."

"I wasn't going to."

Fannon glanced at Shelby, who had ceased ministering to her injured feet and was staring into the fire.

"Has she slept at all?" he asked.

Nils shook his head.

Fannon bit his lower lip, then rubbed his head wearily, running his fingers through his thick black hair.

"What do you think?" he asked. "She going to make it?"

"I don't know."

"Are *we* going to make it?"

"It would be nice."

"We don't dare trust her to pilot the ship," said Fannon.

"No, you're right, of course." They spoke in whispers, so she wouldn't hear. "Unless one of us is watching her."

Fannon nodded. "We could program the computer so that our cryogens could alternate, following her programmed cycle. That way, one of us would be revived every time she was."

"Can we afford that?"

"We're going to have to."

"I'm not worried about the power drain so much as I'm concerned about the situation itself. The ship is her territory. How's she going to feel about one of us looking over her shoulder all the time?"

"You're worried about triggering a paranoid reaction?"

"Frankly, yes. I don't know about you, but I'm rusty when it comes to navigation. We've been so dependent on the pilots, I'm not certain I could catch a mistake if she made one."

"Maybe she'll be all right."

"Does she look all right to you?"

"Well, I mean, shock, you know. . . ."

"She's not in shock."

"You sure?"

"Positive."

"Then what?"

"Your guess is as good as mine. But she is acting very strangely. Almost. . . almost as if she's not all there."

"Can you blame her? I'm not all there myself. When we get back to the ship, we can check her out. Program several navigational exercises into the computer and see how she does. Maybe it'll be just what she needs. You know, being back in her own element."

"Maybe. I—" Nils stopped as Fannon grabbed his shoulder. He was staring just beyond him. Slowly, Nils turned around, his rifle held ready. R'yal was standing just a few yards away, watching them.

Nils stared at the piece of paper he held in his hand. Four words were written on the piece of paper, printed awkwardly, as though by a child's hand. The words were "Take us with you."

R'yal sat awkwardly, staring about him at the interior of the ship. Fannon covered him with his weapon. In spite of Shelby's assurances that R'yal was safe and in spite of the fact that the Shade had been very passive since joining them at their camp, Fannon was taking no chances.

There was some sort of bond between the Shade and Shelby. She had insisted that they bring R'yal aboard the ship with them, and the Shade had not resisted, had in fact seemed quite willing to go. It was an opportunity they could not pass up. Shelby had explained to them that this was the Shade who had taken "the Ones Who Were" away from her. Since the Shade had joined them, Shelby had become more animated.

There was much that still confused the two men, and this was a chance to try and get some answers. They knew, from listening to Shelby's account of everything that had happened to her, that she had achieved a sort of symbioses with the "souls" of the dead Shades, the "Ones Who Were," and that through her, these "ancestors" had some understanding of human beings. R'yal understood their speech and had submitted to an examination. The Shade could not speak. Although there were many anatomical similarities between the Shades and humans, evidently they had evolved along different planes. The Shade possessed vocal cords that might once have been similar to theirs, but they were atrophied. The Shade could produce sounds, but little beyond guttural, animal cries. The Shade was clean, bearing no parasites of any sort, and he had passed the physical for cold sleep, although Nils realized that there was no guarantee that he would survive the experience. Their cryogens had been designed for humans, after all. To an extent, it was possible to program the life-support systems for variables, but it would still be a gamble. A gamble that ColCom scientists would want them to make, but Nils wanted to be certain that the Shade understood the risks. He toyed with the piece of paper in his hand.

"It's remarkable," he said.

"No more remarkable than my understanding of their language," Shelby said. "I couldn't speak it, although I can utter some of the sounds, and if there were a written language for the Shades, I'd be able to write it. Nevertheless, when they were in my mind, I could comprehend the language that they thought at me. K'itar, the . . . elder gestalt among the Shades that were within me, studied me quite closely and carefully. This Shade," she went on, indicating R'yal, "or at least a significant part of him, knows me as well as I know myself. Maybe even better."

"Let's see if I got this straight," said Nils. "This Shade—R'yal—is an individual entity only in the physical sense, right? That is what they refer to as 'the One That Is.' On another level, though, there is no individuality. Rather, there is a gestalt, a sort of cornucopia of Shades that have blended with each other into a variety of aspects that govern the behavior of the physical body . . . a Great Father, a Great Mother, a Great Hunter . . . though none of these aspects are individual entities, either?"

"That's basically it," said Shelby.

"Now I understand what you meant when you said that each Shade was a generation. Or at least I think I'm beginning to understand. It's a staggering concept. I'd like to ask him . . . them . . . a million questions, but I just don't know where to begin."

"It sounds to me like the entire race is schizophrenic," Fannon mumbled.

"From your point of view, you might be correct," said Nils. "But this is normal for them. No wonder this entire mission has been crazy. Their level of sentience defies our definition of the term. We haven't understood anything about them."

He glanced at the piece of paper once again and then looked at R'yal.

"*Why* do you want to go with us?" he asked.

R'yal began to write, very carefully and deliberately. He finished and pushed the paper toward Nils.

"'It is the will of the All Father,'" Nils read. He glanced at Shelby sharply. "The All Father? Does he mean the senior gestalt within him?"

Shelby met his gaze and blinked. "He means God."

"*What?*" said Fannon.

"Wait a minute, Drew," said Nils. "Shelby, what do you mean? They have a religion of some sort?"

She shrugged. "He means God. In the same way that you or I might mean God."

"You're crazy," Fannon said.

"Drew, *please.* Shelby, am I to understand that . . . I don't know. What am I to understand?"

"That seems to be the major unifying factor between the humans and the Shades," she said. "They perceived humans as being blasphemous creatures, because we have never . . . *been.* Do you follow?"

"I think so."

"Well, when they merged with me, they picked up on my conceptions of what God is, or might be. Whatever I know of as being God, whatever I believe or might have believed, whatever I learned about different religions, it was all available to them. The Shades worship something called the All Father, who according to their beliefs is either a part of their physical world or resides within Boomerang itself, the All Mother. Their theology, if you want to call it that, is very primitive. They actually pray to the All Father in much the same way that people pray to God. To them, the All Father is the creator of all things. Including us. They perceive no difference between human conceptions of God and theirs."

"You mean they see our God as being *their* God, too?" asked Fannon, incredulously.

"No, it's the other way around. From what they learned about human theology from me, although I didn't consciously 'teach' them anything, they concluded that humans worship the All Father as well. We just call Him God or Allah or whatever, but they recognized it as being the same cosmic entity, if you will." She chuckled. "To them, we're the lost tribes of Israel."

"I'll be a son of a bitch," said Fannon. "How do you like that for arrogance?"

"No more arrogant than countless human missionaries," Nils replied.

"They regard us as beings created by the All Father, just as they were created by the same entity," said Shelby. "However, they understand that we were created differently. For a purpose. That purpose being to test the people, which is how they think of themselves. To them, life in their hostile environment is a constant challenge, every day a test imposed by the All Father to try their worthiness. We're just another test. We were created alone—as Ones Who Were Not—so that we would have . . ." She paused in thought for a moment. "So that we would have this drive, this hunger to create our technology to enable us to eventually seek out the place where the All Father resides. Our entire culture, all of our technology, our space program, being a Shade equivalent of the Tower of Babel. Only we finally managed to build it high enough. We got to heaven."

"You're not seriously giving them credit for having such a degree of sophistication?" said Fannon.

"That's just my way of phrasing it from what I understand," said Shelby. "Who's to say how sophisticated they really are or might become now? Besides, it's also a question of enlightenment. I didn't say all the Shades perceived the situation in that way. I can only speak for the Ones Who Were within *me*. The Ones Who Were who are now within R'yal."

"Does he . . . do they understand all this?" asked Nils, looking at R'yal.

"Hell, I'm not sure *I* understand it," said Fannon.

"Why not ask him?" Shelby suggested.

"I'm almost afraid to," Nils said. "R'yal . . . do you understand what we're talking about?"

R'yal hesitated for a long while, then began to write. When the message was completed, Nils took the paper.

" 'The All Father is the creator of all things,' " Nils read. " 'The people were created. The places that humans called worlds were created. Humans were created. If the humans were created by a creator not the All Father, who created that creator?' "

Fannon lowered his rifle.

They watched as the swirling blue mist enveloped the Shade. R'yal had shown no fear upon being placed inside the cryogen. The Shade had submitted to the will of the All Father.

"Well, I've done the best I could," said Nils. "I've adjusted the life-support mechanisms to him as best I could. Now I guess it really is up to the will of the All Father, isn't it?"

"I hope to hell he makes it," Fannon said. "I can't wait to see what those button pushers at ColCom will make of him. They'll shit."

"That's one way of putting it," said Nils. He looked at Shelby. "Well, Colonel, what do you think? Can you get us home?"

She smiled mirthlessly. "You think you can trust me?"

Fannon glanced at her sharply.

"I could run a check on you," said Nils, "but I don't really think that's necessary. And I don't want to risk any power drain now that we have our passenger to worry about. You seem fit. And I can't conceive of the Shades having hurt you in any way, not after meeting R'yal. What do you think, Drew?"

"I think I'll be a whole lot happier once we're under way," he said. "I'm content to leave the whole thing up to the All Father. What the hell, He wouldn't have let us get all the way here not to get the job done."

"I wouldn't be too flip about it if I were you," said Nils. "It strikes me that this concept of the All Father and God being the same entity or force is the best chance we have at achieving some sort of cultural link with the Shades. If we can find some way to surmount the problem of their noncommunication with each other's physical selves. Jesus, even the semantics of this whole thing are impossible!"

Shelby stared into the cryogen. "I'll get us home," she said. "Wherever that may be."

Nils frowned. "You're not still—"

"No, no." She shook her head. "You don't have to worry about that. It's just that I *am* home, remember?"

Nils smiled. "That's right, I'd forgotten. But things are different now. They're going to want to talk to you at Col-

Com. And you're not going to be afraid anymore. Things might change."

"They might," she agreed. "I just don't know if I'm ready for Earth. Ask me again when we get there."

"I'll do that," Nils said. He sighed. "I'm tired. I could do with some rest."

Fannon smiled ruefully. "Yeah. Well, nightmare time again. Man, I hate coldsleep. But at least this'll be the final time."

"You're going to resign?" asked Shelby.

"Yeah. I've had enough. Time to retire and become a businessman. How do you feel about going in together on that bar, Nils?"

Nils grinned. "I'll tell you what, let me sleep on it, okay?"

"Deal. C'mon, I'll tuck you in."

As they moved toward their cryogens, Fannon paused by the unit that still held Wendy Chan.

"Hang in there, kid," he said, resting his hand upon the surface of the cryogen. "We'll get you through it somehow." Moments later, Shelby was alone again. She sat down at the controls and took the ship out of orbit, then she plotted the course back to Earth. Perhaps R'yal can help Wendy, she thought.

But who'll help me?

The dome lid of the cryogen retracted and Shelby opened her eyes. Again, she thought. Alone again. She climbed out of the unit slowly, unkinking her muscles, feeling slightly nauseous and dizzy. She hated it.

It was her fourth period out of coldsleep. And there was still a long way to go. She knew that she was going to have to eat something, but she had no appetite. There was work to be done and she would do it, going through the motions like an automaton, feeling an unfamiliar ache inside her. The ache was loneliness.

They had taken that away from her somehow. Perhaps the Shades had done it, perhaps it was her prolonged contact with Fannon and Björnsen, but it wasn't the same any longer. There was no serenity in being alone. There was no solace to be found in working with the computer, in adjusting the course, in checking the life-support systems, in any of the functions she had come to know and love as ship's pilot. There was no comfort in playing chess with the computer or in running any of the library tapes. Looking out the observation port only showed her a vast black emptiness, where before it had been a scene of simple splendor, cold and peaceful.

The mission had changed all of them. Fannon and Björnsen, both misfits in their own respective ways, both men who loved the service, both men who thrived upon the loneliness and the dangers of their work, both wanted out. And the insane ship's pilot, who fled to the void to escape from her anxieties, was now trapped by her own solitude. If she had found sanity and if this was what it felt like, then she desired none of it.

Boomerang seemed to have been a dream. The moment she came back aboard the ship, she had snapped right back into her routine, had felt at home, had thought that finally her ordeal was over. But with everyone in coldsleep, she had discovered that her ordeal had just begun. A new ordeal. An ordeal of emptiness and silence. It was as though she had never left the ship. Everything seemed the same. It was as though none of it had ever happened. Except for just one thing. She couldn't stand being alone. She wanted to go right back into the cryogen, but she knew that she could not. She had responsibilities. Fannon, Björnsen, Chan, R'yal . . . she had to get them back. She could not trust to the ship's computers to do all her work for her. A human agency was needed, a human hand upon the helm.

She thought of a line from a poem by Samuel Taylor Coleridge, "The Rime of the Ancient Mariner."

> Alone, alone, all, all alone.
> Alone on a wide, wide sea!
> And never a saint took pity on
> My soul in agony.

She had never understood the poem. Not completely. What the Ancient Mariner had regarded as a curse, a punishment, had been salvation to her. In many ways, she had come to regard it as her story, only to her being alone was not a purgatory, but a heaven. No longer. They had taken it away. Now she understood the Ancient Mariner. She understood too well.

There was nothing wrong with her. The two men had seen that. She had known that they were concerned about her, that they had felt afraid to trust her to do her job, to bring them back home safely. They had been afraid of what contact with the Shades had done to her. But it was over. She was herself now, only herself, no interlopers in her brain, no aliens sharing consciousness with her, no one to guide her or support her or assuage her pain. Not physical pain; for some reason she could not feel that any more than she could bear being alone. She remembered the injuries she had sustained. She had not felt the rocks cutting into her feet, she had not felt fear crossing the bridge. She did not know why. Perhaps they had taken that from her as well.

People had always taken from her. Her parents had taken from her, had removed themselves from her when she needed them most and had finally completed the task of dying before she ever really knew them. She had been deprived of everything for as long as she could remember. One man had taken more from her than she could afford to give, and she had resolved that it would never happen again. But it hadn't ended. First, Fannon and Björnsen had taken her solitude away from her. Then the Shades had taken her will, a large part of her humanity, and finally, when she was beginning to find a way to survive with them, a way to take for herself for a change, to take their strength and support and, yes, even love . . . R'yal had taken even that. Now what was left?

Where could she go? What would she do? She could no longer function as a pilot. The loneliness bore down upon her like an immense stone, threatening to crush her. The first period out of coldsleep had not been so bad, but as the days wore on, she found herself growing listless and bored, anxious to reenter the cryogen. Something had been missing, but she had not known what it was; she only felt that she had lacked for something. And it wasn't until her second period out of coldsleep that she became aware of what it was.

Companionship.

Having the two men around had made it bearable for a while, but she missed the Ones Who Were, missed them terribly. They had been a part of her. The relationship that she had had with them had been deeper, closer, more intimate and satisfying than any she had ever known. And now they were gone. The third period out of coldsleep had been sheer torture. She had paced about the ship like a caged animal and more than once had considered reviving the others, just so she wouldn't be alone, just so she could hear their voices. But their voices were not the ones she longed to hear. She longed to hear K'itar's voice, to feel his strength within her. She ached for D'lia, the Great Mother, the only "mother" she had every really loved, she knew that now. She pined for the wildness of K'ural, who filled her entire being with a passion for life. And they were forever removed from her. Gone. As close as R'yal's cryogen, but denied to her forever.

She knew only two worlds—the world of a ship's pilot and Boomerang, the All Mother. The ship, once her sanctuary, her womb, now seemed as alien as Boomerang had when she first set foot upon it. She could not go back; the Shades would not have her. And she could not stay where she was, aboard the ship, for if she did, she would wind up just like Wendy Chan.

She forced herself to eat something and was surprised at how ravenous she was. The ship's food did not satisfy. It did not feel the same as that first raw meal she had tasted upon Boomerang. The thought of that eel-like thing was enough to make her salivate. She wished that she could take a javelin and hunt, experience the thrill of killing her own food, feel the warm meat between her teeth as she tore at the flesh.

Mechanically, she started to check the readouts on the cryogens, the first of her many tasks during her period awake. Nils slept soundly; Fannon showed greater activity. He was immobile, but the screen showed that he was dreaming once again, probably the dreams he hated so much. They had that in common, for Shelby's nightmare was a waking one. Wendy Chan was stable, still comatose in coldsleep. Shelby had never even known her. How would it have been if Wendy had not fallen prey to her own mind? She would never have had to take her place, none of it would have happened to her. She would never have set foot on Boomerang and never known the Ones Who Were. She felt anger welling up inside her, but then it subsided. It wasn't Wendy's fault. Besides, even the brief time she had spent being part of the people had been wonderful. She wouldn't have traded it for anything, not even going back to the way things were. If only she could.

She came to R'yal's cryogen. The readings were irregular, but then she had no idea what they should have looked like. At least the unit was not sounding an alert and the readings had not changed significantly from the last time she had checked them. Why had he come?

She opened a locker and removed his weapons. She held the seed-pod hurler in her hands, caressing it lovingly. What had she done with hers, the one she had made with her own hands? She remembered kneeling by the water, carving the wood with her crudely sharpened stone, watching it take form, feeling the warm sunlight on her back and listening to the sounds of the water and the forest. It seemed like a dream. Now there was only silence. She picked up R'yal's javelin, considerably longer and stouter than the one she had carried. She felt its heft. What a thrill it had been when, under the guidance of K'ural, she had faced her first hellhound!

It happened on her way up to the place of mating, along the lower mountain trail. T'lan had sensed the beast and warned her, and K'ural had taken over; a masterful hunter, his aim had been sure and true and the javelin had flown unerringly into the hellhound's heart. And he had made her part of it, she had felt it all with him and voiced her cry along with his. She held the javelin and drew her arm back, then she let it fly.

It sailed across the control room and clattered against the far bulkhead, falling to the deck. It had been a bad throw. She hadn't had K'ural to guide her arm.

Slowly, she went to retrieve the spear. As she bent to pick it up, she felt cold fury building inside her.

How am I going to go back? How can I live? Where is there a place for me on a world that has aged centuries since I first left it?

How could she face ColCom? How could she stand having to relive the whole experience for those scientific ghouls? Why couldn't she have stayed on Boomerang? Even being an outcast among the people would have been preferable to whatever lay ahead of her. And besides, she had always been an outcast. An outcast by choice. And on Boomerang, it would not have been so bad. The Ones Who Were would have been with her. And the only time she would ever have to face another Shade would be if she had to challenge or defend her domain. With K'ural's help, she could have done it. *Would* have done it! And the time of Need . . .

Her breathing quickened as she remembered it. She had never known such excitement. And she *had* found a male to mate with! R'yal. It hadn't been complete, but . . .

R'yal.

It was all R'yal. Cross light-years of space and nothing changed. No male would ever take from her again, but R'yal had taken. Had taken what did not belong to him. Had taken the most vital part of her, had taken her new life. R'yal had condemned her to loneliness. R'yal had deprived her of the Ones Who Were.

Well, she would take them back!

She adjusted the life-support controls to revive R'yal. She would not spend another instant all alone. She would make him return what he had taken. K'itar, K'ural, D'lia, she would have them back. She stood back and watched as the blue mist slowly ebbed away. Her chest rose and fell as she leaned on the spear, staring hard into the cryogen.

Give them back, R'yal.
The chime sounded and the dome lid retracted.
Give them back! I'll make you!
The Shade's eyes fluttered open.
I want what's mine!

Holding the javelin with both hands, she raised it high over her head and plunged it home. R'yal's body arched inside the cryogen, and Shelby was spattered with his blood. The Shade's hand stretched forth in a spasm, fingers splayed wide, searching. . . .

Shelby reached for it.

CHAPTER EIGHT

Fannon took his seat at the semicircular table, facing the four people on the other side. He felt exhausted. Since reviving from coldsleep, he had told his story over and over and over again. It had been a ceaseless parade of nameless faces, sitting behind their computer screens, referring to various segments of the mission tapes, asking him to go over this and that "just one more time for the sake of clarification." After a while, he had started answering like an automaton, not even noticing the person asking the questions. He no sooner became accustomed to one routine than they changed it for another. It was a grueling affair. Questions followed by medical examinations followed by questions followed by psychiatric examinations followed by more questions and more questions and more questions. They had him feeling like a prisoner of war being interrogated by the enemy. He had not seen any of the others, and his questions concerning them always met with the same reply: "In due time, Captain, in due time."

"Captain Fannon," one of the four men said, "my name is Anderson. These other gentlemen are, to my left, Mr. Malik and, to my right, Mr. Jorgensen and Mr. Hermann. We are the Directorate of ColCom."

Fannon sat up and paid close attention. This was definitely not standard operating procedure. Something was wrong.

"To begin with, we would like to apologize for having subjected you to a particularly exhausting and rather unorthodox debriefing procedure. And for keeping you segregated from the other members of your mission team, as well as not answering your questions. It was, however, necessary. Officially, your debriefing is concluded, but we still have some things we would like to clear up. To that extent, I hope you will be patient for just a short while longer, following which we will attempt to answer any questions you may have."

Fannon nodded silently. He waited. Mr. Malik pursed his lips thoughtfully and stared at him for a moment, then spoke.

"For what reason was Captain Björnsen revived from coldsleep during your return journey?" he asked.

"Well, that's not in our report, sir," Fannon said, "but there was some doubt in our minds as to our pilot's abilities to perform her duties properly, in light of all she had been through on Boomerang. Which *is* in our report," he added. "Nils and I worked out a plan to . . . check up on her periodically. Without her knowing. Nils programmed the computer to revive each of us in turn, following every second cycle of her own revival. Our periods awake were to be very brief and only for the purposes of checking our course, the maintenance of the life-support systems, etc. Neither one of us is an experienced pilot, far from it, but we had to do the best we could. I didn't want to mention it because there was really no need. That is, if Shelby . . . well, we both felt that resuming her accustomed duties would be the best thing for her, under the circumstances. And if everything went smoothly, there was no reason to mention that we felt it necessary to check up on her."

But if everything went smoothly, as he had assumed, why had Nils seen fit to mention it to them?

"Then you were also awake during at least a part of your journey?"

"Yes, sir, I was. However, I had assumed that Nils found everything to his satisfaction and that our pilot was performing well, since I was not revived again until we arrived here at ColCom HQ. We did not want to spend any more time out of coldsleep than was absolutely necessary, and we both figured that if there were going to be any problems, they would manifest themselves during the initial stages of the journey. As they did not, I assume that Nils negated the checking procedure following his last period out of coldsleep."

He was tired and confused. What was this leading to? He felt tense and apprehensive.

"I see," said Anderson. "It begins to make some sense now."

"Would you mind explaining it to me then, sir?" said Fannon.

"Not at all. But first, I should tell you that you are not fully aware of the situation. You have not been told everything, but that was for a reason. We had to get certain facts straight. First of all, this is not ColCom HQ."

"*What?* Wait a minute—"

"You wait, Captain. I'm not finished. You are currently aboard orbital station Gamma 127."

Gamma 127? Fannon thought hard. In orbit around . . . Wheeler's World!

"As I see you have surmised, Captain, you are a long way from your destination. Your ship's distress signal was picked up and a rescue mission was sent out from here. What the rescue party found when they came on board your ship led to our decision to come here and investigate for ourselves. You were kept in coldsleep during the time it took us to arrive."

"But . . ."

"If I can anticipate your next question, our presence here is due to the fact that we now have FTL. We have had it for some time now, but there are still only a few ships equipped with the Hawking drive. And it was on our orders that you were kept in coldsleep, along with the other members of your team, until our arrival. It made things more convenient and less of a hardship for you. That is, with the exception of Captain Björnsen. All evidence indicated that he decided to keep Colonel Michaels in coldsleep and took upon himself the task of piloting the ship."

He held up his hand to forestall Fannon's reaction.

"When the rescue mission reached your ship, they found an alien on board. R'yal, the Shade you've mentioned in your report. That in itself was sufficient for us to come.

However, the alien was dead. Captain Björnsen, as you have mentioned, is no experienced pilot. He was suffering from space fever, brought on, no doubt, by the strain of unaccustomed isolation and the task of piloting your ship. He was not entirely lucid, and it was thought, at first, that he had killed the Shade. Please, Captain," he said quickly, as Fannon started to rise from his chair, "allow me to finish. The Shade *was* killed, by a primitive spear thrust into his abdominal region. We subsequently learned that it was your pilot who had killed R'yal. We learned this in a rather unusual fashion, but I will come to that.

"The nature of your debriefing might become clearer to you when you realize that we were faced with a returning team consisting of one woman who was catatonic upon revival, one man suffering from nervous collapse and extensive dissociation, a dead alien and yourself. And then there was Colonel Michaels, who seemed to have gone totally insane. We had to piece together what had happened, and you were our only hope for that."

The man paused, and Fannon took the opportunity to ask about the others. He felt stunned. He had known that there was always the possibility that the Shade would not survive the trip. But that Shelby had killed him . . . *why?* And no sooner had the thought occurred to him than he had his answer. He suddenly realized that he was being spoken to.

". . . all right, Captain?"

"Sir?"

"I asked you if you were all right." Anderson had an expression of concern upon his face.

"Oh. Yes, sir. I'm sorry, it's just that—"

"I understand. This must all come as quite a shock to you. Please try to bear with us."

Of course. Shelby had killed R'yal so that she could merge with the Shades again. It was the only possible explanation. And when Nils had revived . . . damn him. Good old unselfish Nils. He had decided to handle it all himself. From a coldly logical point of view, he had made the right decision. There was no reason for both of them to be awake, but still, he must have known what he was letting himself in for.

"Nils Björnsen will be all right," said Anderson. "It will

take some time, but we've had to deal with space fever before. He is presently in treatment, and there is no cause to worry about him. Lieutenant Chan, on the other hand, poses a greater problem. She is in a state of profound withdrawal. She will receive the best care available, but none of us is qualified to say whether or not she will recover. I'm sorry, but we simply don't know. And we will not know until we can get her to some specialists back on Earth. Until that time, she has been placed in coldsleep once again. It's the most we can do. The remains of the alien have been frozen, so that they can be returned to Earth and studied. As for Colonel Michaels—"

"You know she's merged with the Shades again, don't you?" Fannon said.

"We know very little, Captain," the man named Hermann said. He was slight and had a thick accent. "Pilots have always been unstable individuals."

"What are you saying?"

"A few questions first, Captain. Regarding this form of telepathy possessed by these Shades—"

"Excuse me, sir," Fannon said, warily, "but it was never our conclusion that the Shades were telepathic."

"What of this telepathic contact, then, that you claim they had with Colonel Michaels?"

"I did not *claim* any such thing," Fannon replied, choosing his words very carefully. He had been lulled by their sympathetic tone, but suddenly the memory of the Rhiannon affair was foremost in his mind.

"How would you put it, then?"

"Personally, I never had any evidence of the Shades being capable of telepathy, at least insofar as we understand the term," he said slowly. "They were never in telepathic contact with me, at any rate. And they did have ample opportunity."

"Yet," Hermann continued, "you describe being affected by their presence, feeling certain . . . sensations?"

"True. We concluded that the Shades are capable of a form of . . . empathic projection, if you will. I strongly suspect that this is involuntary with them. That we can sense this projection in much the same way as . . . as an animal can sense fear in a human, for example. We seem to be able to pick up their vibrations, which may be an awkward way of putting it, but it's the best I can do. To a certain type of individual, this could and would be dangerous."

"An individual such as Lieutenant Chan?"

"Yes, sir, I would suspect so. However, there is no definite proof that this is what happened to her. My own personal feeling is that she wasn't strong enough for the rigors of the mission. Making it through training is one thing; actually being able to take it in the field is another."

"Are you saying, then, that her condition is not the result of tele—empathic contact with the aliens?"

"I'm saying that I don't know, sir. But if that is what happened, then I'm certain that it was an accident. The Shades never meant us any harm."

"I remind you, Captain, that this is an official hearing and that your statement is on the record. You intend to stand by that?"

"Yes, sir."

Hermann pursed his lips again and nodded to himself. Then he stared at Fannon pointedly and said, "Captain Fannon, on what grounds do you base your conclusion that Colonel Michaels experienced this . . . merging phenomenon?"

"I—I'm not sure I understand what you mean, sir."

"Well, allow me to rephrase my question, then. Your use of your pilot on your mission was highly irregular and contrary to regulations. Under the circumstances, we have decided that it was justifiable. However, Colonel Michaels *is* a pilot. And it is well established that the stability of pilots is uncertain at best. Colonel Michaels would have been subjected to a great deal of unaccustomed strain, and to an environment from which she had retreated, by choice, when she joined the service. What leads you to reach the conclusion that she experienced merging with the Shades, rather than a psychosis?"

So there it was at last. Just as Nils had anticipated back on Boomerang. They didn't believe it.

"On the grounds that, following her contact with the Shade, Shelby had access to certain information which could have come from no other place."

"In other words, she knew things only a Shade would have known?"

"Yes, sir."

"Such as?"

"That's all in our report, sir. Such as the details of their challenge rituals, their place of mating, their habits, knowledge of the properties of local flora and so forth."

"Yet this was all knowledge that could have been acquired by research and observation, isn't that so?"

Fannon frowned. "What are you trying to say, sir? What do you think we did out there? You think we all went nuts and made the whole thing up?"

"Temper, Captain," Anderson said.

"Temper, hell! Either you're going to accept our findings or you're not, and if you're not, I'm entitled to know the reason why! Look, I don't *know* why Shelby killed that Shade. I mean, I çan take a guess at the motive, but I still don't see why that would have made her kill, for God's sake. You haven't been straight about anything with me, and now you're sitting here and expecting me to give you some sort of rote answers, and I don't even know the rules of this damned game! If Shelby killed R'yal, then he's merged with her. Why don't you have her brought in here? You want to know about the Shades, why not go to the source? Ask R'yal. He's not dead. I don't know what you're trying to get me to say here. If you want to believe that Shelby went off the deep end and developed some sort of split personality, there's not a whole hell of a lot that I can do to prevent it, but I'll be damned if I'm going to help you! We went out there and we found possibly the most unusual race humans have ever come up against and you want to deny it all? For God's sake, *why?*"

Hermann appeared about to reply, but Anderson touched his shoulder and the four of them put their heads together for several moments. When they faced him again, it was Anderson who spoke.

"Captain Fannon, you've been away for a long time. Things have changed in that time. They have changed a great deal. And the nature of those changes affects you and it affects the outcome of your mission. For one thing, now that we have the Hawking drive, the sort of individual who has, up until now, been recruited to pilot our ships is no longer needed. In many ways, Captain, you yourself may no longer be needed. I understand that you have expressed a desire to retire from the service. You certainly have the right to do so, and there is rather a substantial sum of money coming to you, but you may wish to reconsider your decision in light of what we are about to tell you.

"Earth has changed. These changes have affected the human colony worlds as well. For one thing, with the advent of FTL, Earth will be closer to her colonies. For another, things that happen on Earth will have a greater bearing on those colony worlds. It has already happened. I won't go into the full details—you can look those up for yourself—but I will summarize, and possibly you will understand our reasons for what we are about to do.

"For many years now, people have been promised marked advances in anti-agathic research. A drug was developed and was widely publicized in the media as the long-awaited 'immortality pill.' It wasn't quite, but the publicity surrounding the research created intense interest in the drug. The initial experiments looked promising. But as time dragged on, people became impatient. Who wouldn't want to live forever, especially when you've been told that there is a drug that will enable you to do so? Only you can't have it yet. Where there is a demand, there always, sooner or later, comes an outlet of supply. Somehow, the formula was stolen and the drug began to appear on the black market. It was expensive, but what is life worth, after all? There were plenty of buyers. And it was impossible to control, especially because the drug appeared to work. People who should have died did not. Terminally ill patients suddenly recovered. However, in time—and it did take some years—it turned out that the drug was not all it appeared to be at first. Just as the researchers had said, it had not been fully tested. There were dangers. But people with hope in their hearts believe what they wish to believe.

"The drug turned out to have some horrible side effects that did not manifest themselves until years after the treatments had begun. The lifespan was, in fact, prolonged . . . but at a horrible price. Eventually, the body would begin to cannibalize itself, and those who had taken the treatments died horribly. And, even more horrible, the drug resulted in the birth of monster babies. I myself had one in my family. My granddaughter did not survive the experience. It was just as well. The death that awaited her was far more agonizing than dying in childbirth. And the infant was put to death.

"The problem was widespread. The drug had been smuggled out to the colony worlds, as well. The furor that resulted ended in the researchers themselves, blameless though they were, being murdered. And another result of the drug's effects was a massive religious revival. The psychology of the mob is a frightening thing, Captain. People once again began to believe that, as the old saying goes, there are some things that man was not meant to meddle with. They chose to look at what had happened as a punishment from God. That God did not mean for humanity to enjoy eternal life. There is even now a movement, rapidly growing in size, that holds that man was not meant to venture out into space, to colonize other worlds. For obvious reasons, this movement is confined to Earth, yet it is gaining in strength, enough so that it begins to trouble us. Worlds *must* be colonized, but zealots will not understand. They are being fruitful, Captain, and they are multiplying. But the people must have someplace to go. Earth is not room enough.

"And now, Captain, you return to us with the news that there is a sentient race upon Boomerang. A race, moreover, that believes in the All Father. And that, to them, there seems to be no difference between the God that they believe in and the one that has now gained so many zealous followers on Earth and on other worlds. And you tell us that this race does not know death. That only the body dies, but the essential ingredient that makes up a living being survives. The soul, if you will. Survives in a demonstrable fashion, not in some heaven no man will ever know until he dies. Think, Captain, how this news will be received. A race that lives forever. An *alien* race. God has seen fit to deny immortality to humans, yet he has given it to beings who are little more than animals. Yes, yes, Captain, I know that they are, in fact, considerably more than animals, but that is not how it will be perceived. Can you imagine what the effect of your mission's findings will be?

"We believe you, Captain. We accept the findings of your mission. But officially, we do not dare to do so.

There may come a time, in the undetermined future, when it will be desirable for humans and Shades to meet. But that time is not now. And it will not come in my lifetime certainly, and it is doubtful if it will come in yours. No one must ever learn the truth about Boomerang. No one must ever know about the Shades. Those who do know, such as the people who took part in your debriefing, have the highest security clearances. And in spite of that, they cannot be allowed to return to Earth, or to go to any colony world where the knowledge they possess could somehow leak out. They know and understand this.

"We must compel you to secrecy, Captain Fannon. And we cannot allow you to return to Earth. Nor can we allow you access to any of the colony worlds. We do not have the right to do this, we do not have the authority, but we do have the means. That is why I beg you to reconsider your decision to retire and not to take too hard the official evaluation of your mission.

"We are prepared to release the findings of your mission as a routine report that Boomerang is not suitable for colonization. To that extent, we agree with your findings officially. But the official reasons for our findings will be that, contrary to the expectations of those who sent you out upon your mission, Boomerang will not support human life. Nor does it have anything to make it feasible for commercial exploitation of any sort. Its environment is extremely hostile, and caused the death of most of the members of your team. In short, Captain, we will arrange it so that no one will ever learn the truth about Boomerang, or want to question our report. It is my earnest hope, Captain, that you understand our position and that you will cooperate with us."

Fannon sat silent for a long moment, staring at them, feeling stunned. To have come so far, to have gone through hell only to—

"And if I refuse?"

Anderson drew his lips into a thin line. He sighed and drummed his fingers on the table.

"You cannot refuse, Captain. If you do, then you will leave us no alternative. Consider: your ship returned with one member of your team in catatonic withdrawal, with possibly no hope of ever being cured. Another came down with space fever. Still another, the pilot, hopelessly insane, claiming to have been possessed by the spirits of alien beings. By all standards, Captain, your mission was a disaster. Someone must be held responsible. That leaves only yourself. There is also the matter of the murder of a sentient being. Need I say more?"

Fannon looked down at his hands and found that they were shaking.

"No, sir." He looked up at Anderson. "No, I think you've said enough. You've made yourself quite clear."

"I had hoped," said Anderson, "that I wouldn't have to."

"Yes, sir, I'm sure you did."

"I don't blame you for hating me, Fannon. I think I can understand how you must feel, believe me."

"Go to hell. Sir."

Anderson stiffened. "Return to your quarters, Captain. You will find they have been changed for more comfortable accommodations. Regardless of what you might think, we deeply regret having placed you in the position in which you find yourself. We are not villains, Captain. We must do what is best for society. Unfortunately, that forces us to make you the scapegoat. Regrettable, but unavoidable. Nevertheless, we will try to do well by you. Insofar as we are able. Until we decide just how to best accomplish that goal, we will make your stay aboard Gamma 127 as comfortable as humanly possible. You may request anything you wish, and if it is in our power to grant that request, we shall. We are not ungenerous. Once you've had time to think about it, perhaps you'll understand and not judge us so harshly. We care about the people under our command, Fannon. In many ways, they are our children. And when they hurt, *we* hurt. You are dismissed."

Fannon snorted and rose slowly to his feet. He turned and walked toward the door, but stopped just before he came to it and turned back to face them.

"Mr. Anderson, are you familiar with the work of Oscar Wilde?"

Anderson frowned. "No, Captain, I'm afraid I'm not."

"Too bad. I'll leave you with a quotation, though. Something your heartfelt sincerity brought to mind. 'Children begin by loving their parents; after a time they judge them; rarely, if ever, do they forgive them.' " He came to a smart attention and saluted them. "Goodnight, gentlemen."

CHAPTER NINE

It was a spacious room, well furnished and luxurious. Someone had given up his quarters for him, obviously. Fannon didn't think for a moment that it was one of the Directorate. The quarters weren't that luxurious. Still, the carpeting was thick and the walls were actually paneled in mahogany. The furnishings were unusually sculpted, and the lighting could be infinitely adjusted. There was an observation shutter, and the suite possessed all the amenities, right down to a computer console and screen, although Fannon suspected that there would be limits to the information he would be allowed access to and the individuals he would be allowed to contact. He tried it, sitting down at the console, and found himself looking at an officer's face upon the screen.

"Yes, sir?"

Fannon almost switched off, but then he remembered that he was hungry.

"How well are the galleys stocked?" he asked.

"Excellently well, sir. Please feel free to order anything you wish."

"Anything, eh?"

"Yes, sir. I'll be happy to take care of it for you."

"Is that your job, Lieutenant?"

"For the duration of your stay, yes, sir, it is."

"What will the Directorate be eating?"

"One moment, sir, I'll check and see if they've specified

their menu for third mess. . . . Ah, here we go. They will be starting with a pheasant pâté and tortellini, followed by Cornish hen and beef pie. For the main course, there will be roast pheasant with Cumberland sauce and goose with prune and apple stuffing. There will be Tununda salad, salad Niçoise—"

"Hold it, hold it. I don't even know what some of that stuff is."

"In that case, sir, may I be allowed to make a suggestion?"

"Such as?"

"How about some venison, sir?"

"*Venison!*"

"Perhaps with potatoes, green vegetables and spinach salad with mushrooms?"

"I don't believe it. You have venison?"

"Yes, sir. There aren't many deer left, but there is a game preserve in the basement of Colorado near Cheyenne Mountain, where the ColCom Earth base is situated. They are a protected species, but exceptions are made occasionally. The station commander has a fondness for game of that sort, and seeing as how you're from Colorado, sir . . ."

"You mean they're letting me dip into the station commander's larder?"

"Our orders are to provide whatever is available for you, sir. You are on VIP status."

"Whatever is available, huh? How about shore leave?"

"Sorry, sir."

"I didn't think so. Just send the food up."

"We are under orders to make your stay here as comfortable as possible, Captain. If I may be permitted to offer another suggestion?"

"Yes, what is it?"

"Well, seeing as how you have been in the field for quite some time, sir, could I arrange for a dinner companion for you?"

"Yeah, sure, why not? I could do with someone to talk to."

"Very well, sir. Will there be anything else?"

"Yeah. Is there anything in your orders that prevents me from talking to Colonel Michaels?"

"One moment, sir. . . . No, sir, there isn't. Would you like me to patch you through?"

"Please."

"Stand by, sir."

His face disappeared from the screen and was shortly replaced by that of another officer, a lieutenant colonel, judging by his insignia. VIP indeed, thought Fannon. No lower echelons for this security detail.

"Captain Fannon?"

"Yes, sir."

"Lieutenant Colonel Thorsen."

"Sir."

"I am the . . . attaché to Colonel Michaels."

"Yes, sir, I'm sure you are."

The expression on the man's face indicated that he was far from happy with the job. He looked a little rattled, too.

"Before you speak with Colonel Michaels, Captain, I'd like only to tell you that . . . well, naturally, I am somewhat familiar with the situation you find yourself in right now. I was a field officer myself some years ago. I'd just like to say . . . I'm sorry."

It wasn't until that moment that Fannon realized, fully realized, that because of him, everyone connected with their mission was affected. He had been thinking of these men as his watchdogs, but they were now in the same boat as he was, through no fault of their own. Victims of circumstances and the whims of the Directorate, just as he was.

"I understand, sir. I'm sorry, too."

Thorsen nodded silently.

"Can I speak with Colonel Michaels now?"

"Well, that all depends, Fannon."

"On what?"

"On whoever she is at this moment. I've had rather a hard time trying to keep track." He paused. "It must have been a bitch of a mission."

Fannon sighed. "Yeah. I guess it was at that."

Thorsen got up, and a moment later Shelby's face filled the screen.

"Shelby?"

"Hi, Fannon."

She looked terrible.

"How are you?"

She shrugged. "As well as could be expected, I guess."

From the sound of her voice and the look of her, that wasn't well at all.

"What *happened*?"

"Something wonderful. And something horrible. I've got them back, I don't know if you knew. . . ."

"I guessed. But *why*? Why that way? Was it so bad?"

She closed her eyes and nodded. Then she opened them again, but they seemed not to be looking at him.

"Worse than you could imagine," she said. She paused. "You know, you go through life with a sense of who you are, an identity, I guess. This is what you are and you know it, you don't have to hang onto it. It's not as if anyone is going to take it all away. I mean, no matter what happens, you're still who you are, with all your wants and your needs and your . . . They took it all away from me, Drew."

"The Shades?"

She nodded. "I thought everything would be all right, once I was on the ship again. It was my world. *My* world, where I belonged. Only I didn't, not anymore." Her eyes focused on him. She began to weep. "I wasn't a pilot anymore. I couldn't be alone." She licked her lips, and Fannon noticed that her lower lip was trembling. "They . . . they got inside me so deeply. . . . All my life, I've been afraid of letting anyone get close. Anyone who did, they always hurt me. I hurt easily, I guess."

She wiped a tear away and smiled, self-consciously.

"I had everything worked out. I was self-contained. I just built my walls and crawled behind them and I was safe. No one could touch me. I was completely insulated from the world. I had my ship and that was all I needed, all I wanted. Then . . .

"What do you do when everything you are, everything you've struggled to become, just gets turned inside out all of a sudden? They got inside me, through every wall I've ever built, they just went through. And they became a part of me. I never knew it until I found myself alone back on that ship again."

"Shelby . . ." Fannon took a deep breath. "*Did* you kill R'yal?"

She nodded. "I had to have them back. I *had* to. I wouldn't have made it any other way. But I still can't believe it."

"What made you do it?"

"It's not what made me do it so much as what didn't make me *not* do it," she said.

"I don't understand."

"I don't quite understand it all myself. Neither do the Ones Who Were, exactly."

"What have they got to do with it?"

"They're the only reason why I haven't fallen completely apart," she said. "It's more than just survival, Drew. They care. And if they don't completely understand humans, it's not for lack of trying. When . . . when R'yal took them away from me, back at the place of mating, it wasn't R'yal who was responsible. Not the One That Is. It was the Ones Who Were."

Fannon knew that Thorsen might be listening, and he wondered what he was thinking of it all. But then, not having been there, how could he possibly follow their discussion? He could check the mission tapes a hundred times and still not know. He wasn't there.

"R'yal had seen me before," Shelby went on. "I hadn't realized it, but we had seen each other before the time of Need. When it all happened to me, R'yal was the one who should have received them, R'yal was the one who responded to the Call. Only I was there and R'yal hesitated before approaching and . . . then it was too late. The Shades can feel guilt, too.

"The Ones Who Were within R'yal felt that the Ones Who Were in me belonged with them. So they took them. It was what they felt they had to do. There was a wrongness in it to them, just as there was a wrongness in what you saw, from your point of view, with Nils, when you saw me in the place of mating. You took me away, just as they took the Ones Who Were away from me. Only there was no . . . no precedent for what they did. I was still alive. I wasn't dying. There had been no Call. And what was inside me was not all Shade, you see. What they did, they did out of outrage. And they—they drained off part of me, too.

"That's the part I don't fully understand. They've tried explaining it to me, but . . ." She shrugged, helplessly. "The most that I can understand is that after they took the Ones Who Were away from me, I wasn't complete. I didn't know it, though, but a part of me, some portion of my essence, went with R'yal. And T'lan tells me that the part they took away was the essence that makes people different from beasts."

"And so you were able to kill without conscience," said Fannon. "I knew there was something strange about you, but I couldn't put my finger on it. Your weird behavior . . . well, who wouldn't act strange after what you'd been through? But then you didn't seem to feel pain, or fear, for that matter. They took that, did they? What was it like?"

"I don't really know," she said. "At that point, it was as though I was on automatic pilot. I didn't know that anything was missing. But then I wasn't all there. Maybe I just couldn't think about it. I've been running it through my head over and over, and it's all so frightening and confusing. . . ."

"Never mind. It's not important. But it may answer why R'yal came after us. The Ones Who Were within him were exposed to a part of you that they hadn't bargained on. It's as if the tables were turned. Suddenly they were in the same position you were in when the Shades first merged with you."

"Yes. And they felt terrible about what they had done. Only they didn't know how to undo it. If it could be undone."

"Well, it's been undone now," said Fannon.

"And I have to live with it," she said. "I have to live knowing that I took a life."

"But you *didn't* take a life," Fannon said, "not really. R'yal is still alive, within you. You can't think of it in human terms. It's not the same. All right, you killed his body, and maybe you might have caused him a brief instant of physical pain, but he's *still alive*. You've got to hold onto that, no matter what. You can't go on blaming yourself. You *weren't* yourself, were you? You didn't ask for any of this. Surely R'yal knows that. Doesn't he?"

"Isn't it the same?" she asked. "Who are we to say? Just because humans don't have the capability to merge as the Shades do, does that make the killing of a Shade less of a crime than the killing of a human? They're living, *thinking* beings, Drew. R'yal is very strong. I feel his strength with me all the time. I don't know if he hates me for what I've done, I don't know if the Shades can hate, they're so much different than we are, but I do know that he feels . . . well, cheated."

"How do you mean?"

"During life is when the One That Is grows in strength. It's an important stage of their development. R'yal felt that he was meant to be a Great Father one day, or a Great Hunter. He was young for a Shade. He had seen only two times of Need. Drew, I feel like I've killed a child. Oh, I know it's not the same, but there was so much R'yal had left to live for as the One That Is, there was so much growing to be done, and now I took that all away from him. And I know just how much it meant to him because he's now a part of me. It's just so . . ."

She started to break down, and Fannon watched in helpless fascination as her body shivered and began to jerk. He saw Thorsen's hands come into view as he grabbed her to move her away from the screen, and he shouted at the man to leave her alone. Thorsen backed off. There wasn't the slightest doubt in Fannon's mind as to what was happening. Shelby was becoming hysterical, but the Ones Who Were fought with her panic, bringing her back under control. He could see it happening. Her face, which had started to contort, began to relax, as did her body. Slowly, she began to breathe regularly. Her eyes were closed.

"Shelby," Fannon almost whispered. His hands gripped the table, white-knuckled fingers clutching hard. "Shelby, are you all right?"

After a moment, she nodded. She swallowed, then looked at him and bit her lower lip to keep it from trembling.

"Drew, what's going to happen to us?"

Fannon's face was grim. "I don't know."

"They must have told you something."

"What have they told you?"

"That we can never go home again. They explained their reasons, but . . . I don't really know what home is. It's not the same for you, though, is it?"

"Maybe not," he said. "I don't know. I have no idea what they plan for us. They promised to take care of Nils and Wendy. I never really thought much of ColCom's promises, but I think they meant this one. It's gotten too close to home for them. We're real, they've seen us and talked to us, we're not just statistics in some book. We're faces to them now, and they're going to have to be able to sleep at night. But whatever happens, you've got to make it through. You may be the most important human being alive. There's no one else like you. Remember that. Hang onto it. You're somebody now. Somebody they're going to want to know more about. Somebody they *have* to know more about. You're important to them. And you're important to me, too."

She smiled. "You would be better off if you had left me in coldsleep after what happened to Wendy."

"You mean better off not having known you?" Fannon shook his head. "I don't think so. What would the Shades say? It was the will of the All Father?"

"Perhaps it was. Thanks, Drew."

"Yeah. You look tired. Maybe you should get some rest."

She nodded. "I think I will. I'm getting a headache. They're being very active. I guess maybe they need some time to themselves. Will you call me later?"

"You know I will."

"Bye, Drew."

"Yeah. See you later."

The screen flickered and the lieutenant's face appeared again.

"Sorry to disturb you, sir, but since you're finished with your call, I'm informed by the detail outside your door—"

The man looked suddenly uncomfortable.

"It's all right, Lieutenant, I know there's a guard on me."

"I'm sorry, sir."

"Never mind. Forget it. What were you saying?"

"That your dinner's ready, sir. Shall I inform the guard to have it brought in?"

He didn't feel very hungry anymore, but it had been a long time since he ate.

"Yeah, go ahead."

"Sir."

The screen went black. A moment later, the door hissed open and his meal was brought in. Room service. Just like a posh hotel, he thought. When was the last time he had stayed in a posh hotel? Back when he was a rookie, on his first leave. It seemed like several lifetimes ago. They set his table very quickly and efficiently, all without a word to him. Orders, most likely. He realized that everyone who talked with him would be in danger of sharing his fate. He didn't mind, under the circumstances. Don't touch the leper. The table set, the meal ready, they came to attention and saluted him. He returned their salutes halfheartedly, and they left. He got up and walked over to the table. Well, it smelled good, at any rate. Perhaps he was hungry after all. As he sat down, the door hissed open once again. He looked up to see who it was.

"Captain Fannon," she said. "How nice of you to invite me. I've never tasted venison. What is it like?"

"You've hardly said a word throughout the meal," she said. "Is it me?"

"Yeah, I guess so. You haven't touched your food."

"I'm afraid I don't like it very much."

"That's all right. Some people don't. It tastes too gamy for them."

"Would you prefer someone else?"

"What?"

"If I'm not your type, I could have them send someone else. What sort of woman do you like?"

He stared at her. She was very beautiful. Dark hair, cut short, green eyes, high cheekbones, very full lips. She was tall and slender, with an athletic build. She had a calm, self-possessed air about her. She looked him in the eyes when he spoke to her.

"It's not that," he said.

"Oh? What is it, then?"

"You're not a civilian?"

"I'm a second lieutenant."

"Why are you doing this? Did they order you to?"

She smiled. "Oh, I think I see. No, Captain, it's my job. Second Lieutenant Christine Vargas, Courtesan Corps."

"Courtesan Corps! You're joking."

She shook her head, a bemused expression on her face.

"You mean to tell me they're actually recruiting women for . . ."

"Men, too. You *have* been away a long time, haven't you?"

"I don't believe it."

"Why not? It's eminently practical."

"Jesus. Yeah, I guess it is, at that, but why would you . . ."

"Oh, really, Captain. Because I enjoy it."

"Sorry."

"Don't be. I like my work. It suits me. I'm omnisexual by nature, and it's a very pleasant way to make a living. I don't have to work very hard at all."

"What did they tell you about me?"

"No more than I needed to know. Your name is Captain Drew Fannon, you've just returned from a mission the details of which we are not to discuss, and I'm to be especially nice to you. That won't be difficult at all."

Fannon refilled his glass with baharri. It was a good brew, particularly strong.

"Suppose I try to talk to you about the mission? Or get drunk and do it accidentally?"

"I will be interrogated later, Captain. They'll wire me and ask me questions. Nothing intimate, I'm sure, just did you discuss your mission with me. They made it quite clear to me that I was not to know. For my own good. Judging by the way you've been putting that brew away, I'd say you were a man who doesn't get drunk unless he wants to. And if you try to discuss your mission with me, I will stop you."

"How?"

"By rendering you unconscious. You don't have to worry, though, I won't hurt you. You seem to be a very important man."

"*You'll* render *me* unconscious?"

"Careful, Captain, your ego's showing."

"Maybe. But I don't think that you could do it."

"Would you care for a demonstration?"

"By all means."

She smiled and stood. They moved away from the table.

"Okay," said Fannon, "show me."

"One moment." She went over to the door and knocked twice. It hissed open and she spoke briefly to the guard outside. Then she came back in to face him. "Would you care to make the first move?"

"All right. The destination of our mission was—"

Her foot almost connected with his solar plexus. She was very fast indeed. He blocked the kick more by reflex than as a result of conscious action. She came right back at him, with a combination of roundhouse kicks, three off the same foot, one to the groin—a feint—and two more to the temples, a roundhouse to the left, reverse roundhouse to the right. He blocked two of them, but the third connected. It felt like a gong going off inside his head.

He staggered, then snapped off a side kick that threw her clear across the room. She hit the wall, bounced back and immediately came back at him with a series of spinning-wheel kicks and elbow-strike combinations, which prevented him from moving in to try to trap her while her back was turned to set up for the next kick, which wasn't for very long at all. He could barely follow it. He backed away, blocking madly, looking for an opening. There wasn't one. So he dropped and tried a sweep. It worked, and she went down. He lunged on top of her, going for a choke hold, but she broke it and in the same motion brought both palms together with his head between them. He heard the gong again. He swung wildly and connected with her jaw.

Then they were both on their feet, and he saw that there was blood coming from her mouth.

"Okay," he said, slightly winded and dizzy, "that's—"

A piledriver hit his chest. She had a method of delivering a side kick that made it very difficult to see it coming. Instead of pivoting, she would bring her rear foot alongside her front one sharply and, in the same motion, snap the front foot out, using the momentum. Nothing about the position of her body gave the kick away. She hit him with three more before he was able to block it. When number four came at him, he used an outside block, sweeping his arm down and catching the kick with his forearm, using its momentum to brush it aside and spin her around, exposing her back. Then he moved in with a punch to her kidney. Even as she cried out and took the punch, she brought her elbow around fast and clipped him on the temple. Another gong.

He wasn't able to recover from that one quite quickly enough. He caught a palm-heel strike to the chin which straightened him out, a spearhand thrust to his solar plexus that doubled him over, and a chop to the back of the neck that laid him out. The floor came up hard.

"Bastard," she said, holding her side.

When he came to, she was leaning up against the wall, still clutching her side and watching him. He got up to his hands and knees.

"Son of a bitch," she said, in a low voice. "*Damn*, you hit hard." She raised a napkin to her mouth and wiped some blood away. "They didn't tell me that you knew karate. You're very good, but you're out of practice."

He struggled to his feet. His neck felt sore and he had a tremendous headache.

"Are you all right?" she asked.

"Yeah. Yeah, I'm okay. I'm sorry. I guess I got a little carried away." He let his breath out slowly. "You proved your point."

"You feel any better now?"

"A little. How'd you know?"

"It's my job, Fannon. You had to hit somebody. I hope you've worked it out now. I'm not in the mood for another round."

He sat down and poured them both a drink.

"How's your side?"

"Sore. No permanent damage, though." She took the drink and winced as she brought the glass up to her mouth. Her lip was cut and swollen.

"It really is too bad," she said. "It might help if we could talk about it. But we can't."

"Yeah."

"Why don't you take me to bed, Drew? It's better than beating the shit out of each other."

Later, as he lay beside her, his head buried in her shoulder, she stroked his hair. She could feel the damp of his tears against her skin. When he feel asleep, she quietly slipped out of bed and dressed. Walking softly, she went to the door and knocked. It opened and the guard let her out.

"You all right, Christine?" he asked.

She nodded. "Yes, Jerry, I'm all right." She looked back into the room, at Fannon's sleeping body. "I'm not sure if he is, though. I guess this job isn't quite as easy as I thought it was."

Jerry didn't understand.

CHAPTER TEN

Fannon awoke with a start. He had been trying to wake up for some time, it seemed to him, but some dreams don't let go too easily. Especially nightmares. This one had been an old friend.

He was a boy, back in Colorado, living on the fourteenth level of Colorado Springs with his parents. His father worked in city maintenance and his mother was a sergeant in the police department. He was their only child, all they were allowed. Colorado had been one of the first states to impose population-control statutes. They spoiled him rotten. At least once a year, his father took him hunting in the basement, and every weekend, if he had behaved himself, they would take him to the Cheyenne Mountain spaceport to watch the shuttles taking off. For as long as he could remember, he had wanted to go to space. He would watch the shuttles winging their graceful way out to the orbital stations and dream of being aboard. His father had always felt that it was merely a youthful fantasy that he would outgrow, but his mother had known better.

"I know it seems terribly romantic to you, Drew, but you know, being a spacer can be very lonely."

"Oh, Ma, how can it be lonely? Being aboard a ship, a real ship, with a crew, going out to explore strange new planets, how can it be lonely?"

"Those flights take a very long time, Drew. Just think, if

you went aboard one of those ships, and if something awful didn't happen on your journey, by the time that you came back, why, everyone you know would be long dead. Your father and me, all your friends, everyone. And if you were a member of an exploratory team for ColCom, then the crew would be very small indeed. And you'd never really *see* space, you'd be in coldsleep. You would be revived when you arrived at your destination, where the work would be very hard and dangerous, and when it was finished, you'd go into coldsleep once again."

"Then I'll be a pilot. I'll be the one who flies the ship."

"That's the loneliest job of all," she said. "No one to talk to but the ship's computer, a machine. And flying a ship isn't really as glamorous as you think. It's pushing buttons, doing tedious chores. It's just a dull routine. Haven't you ever spoken to your friends about it? Don't you know what they say about pilots?"

"Yeah, I know. Everybody says that they're insane. But I don't believe it. They just say that because if they didn't, then everybody'd want to be one."

"But it's true, son. It takes a very special sort of person to be the pilot of a ship for ColCom. A person who can stand being alone for the rest of his life. That isn't normal, Drew. You're not like that, I know you. You need people, Drew."

"Ahh, I'll trade people for space any old day."

His mother would smile wistfully and say that perhaps when he was older he'd understand.

But when he was older, he understood only about pilots. By then, he knew that he didn't have what it took to be a pilot. But that was no longer what he wanted. He came home one day to announce, at dinner, that he had enlisted in the service, and that he had chosen ColCom as his branch and been accepted as a cadet at the academy. His father had been shocked, then furious. And his mother had just sat silently and cried.

He saw them a great deal while he was a cadet, since the academy was located right in Colorado Springs. He always came home for leave, while the others partied. He had no need of parties. There would always be time for that sort of thing. But he knew that once he went to space, it would be the last time he ever saw his parents. Although she never said anything, he knew that his mother always hoped, secretly, that he would be washed out, but he graduated at the head of his class. And, as a rookie, those early leaves at home were brutal. It was like coming to a wake. His own. After a while, he stopped coming. When he was to board his shuttle to depart to the station, to be briefed on his first mission, they were not there to see him off. He had waited for them until the last possible moment, but they hadn't come. Perhaps it was for the best.

It was during that first voyage that the nightmare came to him for the first time. He recalled, deep within the dream of coldsleep, a dream so vivid that it seemed more real than any dream that he had ever had, more real than life itself, his childhood, his days of watching shuttles flying to the stations. He recalled his mother telling him about the loneliness of space and of the misery of pilots. And, in his dream, he *was* a pilot, wandering through an old and shattered derelict, its hull ruptured, showing gaping holes that looked out upon the vast black emptiness. There was no sign of life aboard the vessel, there were no lights, no sounds, no activity of any sort. He walked through the ship, protected by his suit, through some manner of ethereal fog that covered everything like shifting cobwebs. The flight couches were torn loose from their fastenings, the instruments were broken, the dials and screens all shattered in a thousand fragments. And as he passed the cryogens, the blue mist inside seemed to beckon somehow, to attract him like a magnet, exerting an inexorable pull. He moved toward the first unit and he looked inside. And, as he looked, the blue mist seemed to shimmer and dissolve, to reveal the body of his mother, dressed in her police uniform. And she was mummified.

Sometimes the dream went on forever. He would walk endlessly through that empty, battered ship, drifting aimlessly in space, knowing that at the end of his walk, he would come to those cryogens and he would look inside. And he would fight against it. In his dream, he tried to will himself to walk through the rupture in the hull, to propel himself through that jagged opening to hurtle into space, anything but to look inside that cryogen. But always he kept walking, trying to will his feet to become paralyzed. But then he'd take a step. And then another. And another. And the cryogens would grow closer, ever closer.

Fannon sat up in bed, putting his feet on the floor. He bent over, elbows resting on his knees, hands dangling limply.

How would the Shades have put it—the will of the All Father? He had been destined for this. There would never be that spacer bar, where old men could come and swap stories of their adventurous young days, exaggerating feats of bravery, telling lies about discoveries they'd made, crying in their brew. It was not to be. Back on Rhiannon, when all hell had broken loose, he had sworn that if he lived he would retire. He could have done so then. But with Rhiannon far behind, the life no longer seemed so frightening. Just one more mission, he had told himself. One more, so I don't leave with a bad taste in my mouth, so no one can say that Fannon lost his nerve. Just one more mission, then bow out with grace. And he had gone out on that mission. And then one more. Just one more. Always there was just one more, until retirement became some vague dream, something that would happen when he was too old to go out on the surveys. On Boomerang, all that had changed. Yet now that he was ready to retire, longing to, they wouldn't let him. There was no escape.

"The time has come for you to leave us, Captain."

Fannon looked up at Anderson and smiled. "You say that as though you were sorry to see me go."

"I *am* sorry to see you go, Captain Fannon. That may sound insincere to you, but nevertheless, it's so. I wish there were some other way."

"Yeah. So do I."

"You may remember, Captain, that the last time we spoke, you quoted to me from the work of Mr. Oscar Wilde. I decided to check the library tapes, and I chose one of his shorter works to read, on your recommendation. By chance, it turned out to be quite appropriate. It was an essay written from personal experience, while Mr. Wilde was in prison. I found it to be quite a moving piece. It was titled *De Profundis*. Permit me to return you quotation for quotation. I took the trouble of copying it down.

" 'Society, as we have constituted it, will have no place for me, has none to offer; but Nature, whose sweet rains fall on unjust and just alike, will have clefts in the rocks where I may hide, and secret valleys in whose silence I may weep undisturbed. She will hang the night with stars so that I may walk abroad in the darkness without stumbling, and send the wind over my footprints so that none may track me to my hurt: she will cleanse me in great waters, and with bitter herbs make me whole.'

"It may well be, Captain, that society does not have a place for you. You are of a breed that left that place behind to seek out new ones of your own. You have done this in the service of society, and we may seem ungrateful, but stop and ask yourself—did you not do it for yourself?

"You're still a young man, Fannon. You have your whole life ahead of you. A twist of fate has led you to your present predicament, and you're bitter because you feel that you are being punished unjustly. You can look at this two ways. You can choose to think of it as exile, if you wish. It's true, we won't allow you your own way, but would you be really happy in retirement? Would you be content? What would you do? You're far to young to live for memories. That is an avocation more appropriate to someone of my age. No, Fannon, you're a spacer. It's in your blood. As I said, you can look at it two ways. Even in prison, feeling pity for himself, Mr. Wilde knew that the time would come when the burden of his sorrow would be lifted from him.

"Is sorrow really what you feel, Captain? Isn't it resentment? The second way in which you can consider your own future is the one I would suggest to you. And that is as an adventure.

"Yes, Captain, an adventure. We are not yet ready for the Shades, but in time, I'm sure we will be. I've spoken with the Ones Who Were, when Colonel Michaels sat where you are sitting now. I won't pretend to understand all that I heard. But I was fascinated. There is something electrifying about Shelby Michaels now. She radiates a . . . a charisma unlike anything I've seen before, even in her misery. It may be this empathic projection phenomenon you spoke of, I don't know, but whatever it is, it's incredibly compelling.

"We must learn about the Shades, we *must*. And Shelby Michaels is our key. I have given a great deal of thought to this and discussed it with my colleagues. The Shades were able to merge with her. And it has not destroyed her. Instead, it seems to have made her stronger, something more than what she was. To see her records, and to see her now, it is almost impossible to believe that she is the same person documented in the files. And, in point of fact, she's not.

"We are giving you an FTL ship, Fannon. Our own, in fact. We have already started to refit it somewhat for your journey, to provide it with the equipment you will need. We can afford to wait for another to take us back; the wait will not be long. I promised you that we would see to the welfare of your fellow team members. Lieutenant Chan will be returning with us, and I give you my word that nothing will be spared in our efforts to make her well again. And, according to your own mission tapes, there is nothing that she knows that can be of any danger back on Earth once she recovers. Captain Björnsen can be treated here. In fact, he is already making progress. And once he is fit again, he will be joining you."

"Joining us where?" asked Fannon.

"At a unique research facility, Captain, which you will help to design and construct. After all, who is more qualified?"

"Not on Boomerang?"

"Yes, Captain, on Boomerang. The fact that we are giving you an FTL ship for the mission should underscore its importance to you. Your pilot will be Lieutenant Colonel Thorsen. Certain personnel already familiar with the details of your mission will be accompanying you. You have an important task ahead of you. Boomerang will be the site of a top-secret research installation. You will be provided with every possible modern convenience. Lieutenant Colonel Thorsen will assist you in setting up your initial base, and then he will return to pick up further needed materials and additional personnel, once they are selected. It will not be as before. This time you will have more company, and you will be armed with information. I expect you to gather more. As much as possible. I expect that, in good time, you will be able to establish quite a comfortable home there. Not quite the retirement you may have had in mind, I agree, but in effect, you will have an entire world for your estate. A far from lamentable state of affairs, Captain. And you will be performing a valued service for humanity. I congratulate you, Captain Fannon. And I wish you well."

Thorsen welcomed him aboard the FTL ship *Wanderer* wearing new insignia.

"I've been promoted," he said wryly. "They made me a full bird colonel so that I could be mission commander. Aren't you impressed?"

"Gee, I'd better salute, huh?"

Thorsen laughed. "I may be a lifer, Fannon, but I'm not a military asshole. My first name's Jacob. My friends call me Jake. Welcome aboard."

Fannon nodded glumly. "Thanks. Most of my friends just call me Fannon. Though I don't know if 'friend' is the right word to use, under the circumstances. Because of me, you're now a lifer in more ways than one. Looks like you're really stuck. I'm sorry, Jake."

"Ahh, forget it. It's not your fault. In a way, it's mine."

"How do you figure that?"

"They told me that there was a top-secret to-do and that they needed me. They said it would involve a great risk. Like an idiot, I volunteered. I thought I was going to get an honest-to-God mission, which would have been a welcome change from playing chauffeur to the Directorate. After all, it was what I had joined up for. Being pilot for the Directorate ain't much fun. They spend most of their time at the HQ and I spend most of my time as an attaché, which is a fancy term for desk jockey. So I volunteer for this top-secret assignment and find out that I'm to baby-sit Colonel Michaels. A real thrill.

"In point of fact," he continued, "it was. She scared the piss outta me at first, but that woman's really something." He paused, nodding to himself.

"Yeah, she is at that," said Fannon.

"Anyway, it looks like I'm going on a mission after all," said Thorsen. "So I can't complain."

"Only they're scared," said Fannon. "So damn scared of something they don't even understand that they're not letting you come back."

"Well, that's not completely true," said Thorsen. "I will be making a few flights while the base is being constructed, but after that, it appears that Boomerang is going to be my permanent home. It could have been much worse, though. I had all sorts of ideas about where they might have sent me—there are all sorts of hardship posts now. I had visions of myself ending up on some orbital research station above an uninhabitable planet. But instead they're sending me out on an honest-to-God mission, to a habitable planet with a sentient race. A real mission, a challenge."

"It doesn't bother you that there's no coming back?"

Thorsen shrugged. "There's not a hell of a lot I can do about it, is there? Sometimes you have to play the cards you're dealt."

"Yeah, well, I'd like a new deck, myself."

They had been walking as they spoke, and they came to Thorsen's cabin. "Stateroom" would have described it more accurately. Fannon whistled.

"Jesus. Talk about traveling in style!"

"You're got one just like it," Thorsen said. "Come on in, have a drink. Hear you like baharri."

A moment later, they were both sitting in comfortable chairs, quaffing the potent black brew. It was hard to believe that they were aboard a ship capable of traveling faster than light, a ship that would take him to a destination from which there would be no return.

"I feel sorry for you, Fannon," Thorsen said. "Don't get the wrong idea, I don't pity you, but I do feel sorry for you. It's a shame the way things turned out for you. I understand you wanted to retire?"

"Yeah. I've been saying that for years, but this time I really meant it. It was going to be quits for sure. Funny, isn't it, how things turn out?"

"I suppose so. You never can tell how things are going to go. But you should be used to that."

"I never got used to being treated like a robot. A piece of expendable property."

"You don't much like ColCom, do you?"

"Whatever gave you that idea?"

"I have a feeling that your dislike does not stem from recent events alone."

"No, they've always had a warm spot in my heart."

Thorsen was summoned on the intercom.

"Come on, I'll show you to your cabin. We'll talk again. You should come on up to the bridge, once we get underway. You've never seen one of these fly, have you?"

"No, I haven't. I'll take you up on that. Thanks."

"My pleasure."

"You know, Jake, I can't get over the way you're taking all of this. I just don't understand it."

"No? Well, look at it this way, Fannon. It's an opportunity."

They parted company at the door to Fannon's cabin. Fannon watched him going back toward the bridge. Then he went inside.

"Drew!"

"Shelby!"

They stared at each other stupidly for a long moment. Too long.

"Thorsen didn't tell me that you were aboard already."

She nodded. "I've got the cabin next to yours." She indicated their surroundings with a brief sweep of her arm. "Some ship, isn't she?"

"Yeah. Beats hell out of what I'm used to."

"It feels very strange, being aboard a ship that isn't mine."

Fannon sat down beside her.

"You seem better," he said.

"Why not? Part of me is going home." She smiled ruefully.

"Yeah, I wanted to ask you about that."

"It's becoming easier," she said. "Which doesn't mean it's easy, just less frightening now."

"How are the Ones Who Were?"

"Would you like to ask them?"

"Uh, I'm not quite sure I'm ready for that yet. Can't you tell me?"

"I can. They're pleased to be going home, but they're sorry that the humans have rejected them. And they're confused about the nature of this mission."

"They're not alone. Shelby, I . . . I don't know, something's different this time. About you, I mean. You seem different from the first time you merged with them. More . . . more yourself, if you know what I mean."

She nodded. "That's the part that isn't becoming any easier. I don't have any control over it."

"You mean they're liable to take over at any time?"

"No, not in the way you mean," she said. "The Ones Who Were within me before know me better than the Ones Who Were within R'yal. That synthesis is still taking place. There is the merging within the merging. K'ural and D'val, for example, and K'itar and T'ran. There can only be one Great Hunter, one Great Father, and so on down the line."

"You mean it's like a power struggle between R'yal's ancestors and yours? What am I saying? I don't mean—"

She smiled. "Yes, I know. It is hard to put it into words, isn't it? You understand better than anyone else, though. Thorsen just gave up. The Directorate kept trying to see it in human terms, and of course that isn't possible. No, it's not really a power struggle, though that's as close a way of putting it as I can think of. It's more like . . . if I was a Shade, it would all have been resolved by now, but I'm not, so that's a large part of the problem. There has to be a merging between the Ones Who Were within R'yal and the Ones Who Were within myself. That should have happened when R'yal took them away from me, but there was nothing normal about that situation. It happened in the middle of the time of Need, and on top of that they drained off part of me as well. There were too many complications, not the least of which was R'yal, the One That Is. Rather, the One That Is then. The one who was the One That Is?"

"I get the idea," said Fannon. "I know, it's tough to talk about. I'm managing to keep up, though just barely. I don't even want to think about what's going on inside there." He tapped her head, then placed his hand on her shoulder. "What I want to know more than anything else is, how does Shelby Michaels fit into it? I'm getting the distinct impression that I'm talking to *you*, without any part of *them* interfering. But they're there and they're a part of you. What are *they* doing right this second?"

"I'm not completely sure," she replied.

"Is that good or bad?"

"How should I know?"

"You're not helping me."

"I can't even help myself. All I know for certain is that the synthesis is not complete yet. And I'm not sure how I fit into that. I am the One That Is, to them. But I'm still Shelby to myself, which part seems stronger at times than they are."

"You mean you're fighting them?"

"Well, in a way, I guess I am. It's difficult. I can hold onto myself better than I could before. I have more of them inside me than I did the last time, so it's a little stormy. I can't keep it up for long, but I've got to come up for air once in a while."

"You mean sublimate the Shades? How do they feel about that?"

"They seem to understand the need. Some of them do, anyway. R'yal is something of a problem. He's strong, and he's resisting merging with the gestalt. I think it's mostly my fault. I've thrown everything completely out of balance. I've been wondering if this is how people with split personalities must have felt."

"What's going to happen when they finally settle down?"

"Assuming that they will. I don't know, Drew. All I know is that it's not like last time. It's different. Not really scary different, just confusing different. But I'm happy about it, whichever way it finally turns out. I know it probably sounds crazy, but I'd rather be this way than the way I was."

"What do you think of Thorsen?" Fannon asked, changing the subject abruptly.

She shrugged. "I really haven't had much time to think about him, all things considered." She frowned, seeing the expression on his face. "Why?"

"He bothers me. He's got a few more flights to make, between Boomerang and wherever, and then he's going to be stuck there for the remainder of his life, most likely, compliments of our Directorate and their paranoia. And he's taking it all too damn calmly. Dammit, *nobody's* that much of a fatalist. I never was able to buy that old chestnut about 'ours not to reason why.' He's looking at this whole thing as though it were just an ordinary mission. We're being *marooned* on Boomerang, for God's sake!"

"I know," she said softly. "But it just doesn't bother me. Not like it bothers you, anyway. I wish there was something I could do."

"What the hell *is* there to do?" Fannon said bitterly. "When I found out they wouldn't let me go, I almost went crazy. There was one night when I—" He thought of Christine and left his statement unfinished. "I was actually tempted to try to break out somehow. Thought perhaps I could overpower the guard, grab his gun. But then what? Grab a shuttle down to Wheeler's World, assuming I got that far? They'd be waiting for me when I came down. Hijack a ship? Ridiculous. There's no chance. And there's no way out. None whatsoever."

"I'm sorry, Drew."

"*God*, I don't want to go back there! It's driving me crazy. And Thorsen actually seems *happy* about it! It just doesn't make any *sense*."

Shelby's eyelids fluttered and she clutched her head.

"What is it?"

"Nothing. I'll be all right."

"What do you mean, nothing? You don't look all right."

"It's okay, Drew, really." She didn't seem to be in physical pain, but she appeared to be on the edge of collapse. "There's nothing you can do. I'd better go back to my cabin."

"It's them, isn't it?"

She nodded. "I'll see you later. I've got to get some rest."

She almost staggered from the room. The door shut and Fannon was left alone.

CHAPTER ELEVEN

There was a crew of forty-five aboard the *Wanderer*. Fannon had been shocked to learn that until he realized that these were the people who were doomed to exile as a result of having, in one way or another, been exposed to too much information while in the process of debriefing the mission team. He had not realized that there were quite so many of them. All but a very small handful of these people were already in coldsleep as he boarded. They were not needed as crew for the journey and so were stowed safely out of the way. They would not dream for long, but he would not be seeing any of them until they arrived at Boomerang.

He wondered how those people would react to him when that time came. He wouldn't blame them if they hated him. True, it was through no fault of his own that he had caused them to forfeit the company of other human beings except those who were to journey with them, but had he not arrived, they would not now be in their present position. No, if they bore him any grudge, he would understand. It would not make things any easier, but he would understand. He could not expect them to direct their feelings against the ColCom Directorate. They would be far away and out of reach forever. But Fannon would be handy. A whole world for your estate. Those had been Anderson's words. That pompous, insufferable hypocrite. But then he ran true to form for the men who guided ColCom. If, years ago, following the mission on Rhiannon, they had been ready to wipe out an entire race and were prevented from it only by the economics of the situation, it followed that it shouldn't bother them too much to send a handful of their minions off to a world from which there would be no return.

What really disturbed him more than anything else was Thorsen's calm acceptance of his fate, in fact, his joviality in the face of it. The man was older than Fannon, perhaps by ten or maybe even twenty years; with him it was hard to tell. Of average height, Thorsen was a stocky man, husky, though not as powerfully built as Fannon. He was fit, but his somewhat undemanding life-style to date had allowed him to put on some excess weight. Weight he would soon lose on Boomerang, thought Fannon. His hair was gray and his face wore a deceptively grave expression, which his easy grin dispelled so quickly that it took some getting used to. And the other members of the crew who were awake all treated Fannon courteously, without the slightest hint of anything that seemed to be resentment. They all went out of their way to give him privacy, which on a ship of that size was not difficult at all, but they certainly did not avoid him.

Had things really changed so much? Had those who served in ColCom finally been reduced to a status of subservience akin to that of worker ants? ColCom says go and they go. Was it as simple as that? In his case, there had been nothing he could do about it, but surely forty-five people could have staged some sort of effective protest against the order that exiled them. Perhaps not. He didn't know what they could have done, short of a mutiny, but it galled him that they had all stoically accepted the decree of the Directorate without even the slightest twinge of regret. There was such a thing as devotion to duty, but this was just too hard to believe. He was going to have to live with all those people. How would he be able to live with them if he could not understand them?

And then there was Shelby, who continued to change before his eyes. She still looked the same, although she began to regain her color and she seemed to tire less easily, but the change was obvious in her behavior. He could almost see the degree of influence the Ones Who Were exerted upon her. Yet, as she had said, it was different from the way it had occurred the first time. She was not simply a puppet whose strings were being pulled by a confused and frightened clan of aliens. No, this time there was a sureness about her that had not existed that first time back on Boomerang. They spent a great deal of time together, talking. And Fannon wondered why he had never realized before how beautiful she was.

Perhaps because before she hadn't been so beautiful. Physically, nothing about her had changed. She had never been what could be called gorgeous, or even pretty, though she was not unattractive. It was a change that could only be attributed to the merging.

She had taken on some indefinable quality that enabled her to project an aura of incredible self-containment. Fannon couldn't put his finger on it. It wasn't in the way she moved, though even that had changed. There was now a sort of languid grace in her slightest movement, an animal awareness of her physical self, not conscious, but there nevertheless. It wasn't in the way she spoke or in the way she acted. Perhaps, Fannon thought, it was in the things she *didn't* do. There was still a great deal of the old Shelby present, the pilot who lived most of her life in loneliness, but the change was that now there was no fear of other people. He had seen that disappear on Boomerang, but he had not fully noticed what it had developed into until now. In losing her fear of other people, Shelby had also lost the normal sense of awkwardness that most people have around each other. She was not uncomfortable with silences; she felt no need to "make" conversation. Nor did she shy away from it. In fact, her direct awareness of anyone who spoke to her had a disconcerting effect upon many of the crew. Other people did not infringe upon her space; rather, she dominated theirs in such a subtle and surely unconscious fashion that an attempt at conversation would soon sputter and be broken off with a mumbled excuse about duties to be performed or some such dodge. And yet these same people who found themselves feeling insecure in her presence would return to speak with her again, making diffident overtures of friendship.

In speaking with her, Fannon became aware of how she

never looked away from him, as she so often used to do. In fact, he could recall a time when she had been unable to meet his eyes. Now, as he spoke, she would sit quietly and listen, drinking him in, it seemed. And she *listened*. It was that, probably, more than anything else, which so disconcerted at first. Most people didn't listen. They merely heard while they awaited their own chance to speak. With Shelby, whoever spoke to her was centerstage, directly in the spotlight of her presence. She made one painfully aware of what was being said. She was so aware of others that she made them ultra-aware of themselves. It was something they were not accustomed to, and once the initial shock of the experience wore off, it produced an overwhelming feeling of euphoria. She attracted others as a magnet gathers iron filings. She made them feel good.

The synthesis was taking place with astonishing rapidity. It was something Fannon was aware of more than the others were, for he knew her far better than they did. As he knew the Shades. Without losing any of her own individuality, she began to take on more and more Shade characteristics. It was a growing process. Her physical senses seemed to magnify. Perhaps they actually improved, perhaps it was just that the Shades enabled her to use them with a greater degree of finesse, Fannon wasn't sure. She would know he was behind her, for example, long before he thought her capable of hearing his approaching footsteps, and she would know that it was he and not Thorsen or one of the others. Once he came to call on her in her cabin and she asked him to come in, her voice inviting him via the intercom before he had even knocked upon her closed door. And another time, when he had difficulty sleeping, he went for a walk and heard her moving about inside her cabin. Upon entering, he had spoken to her for some minutes before he suddenly became aware that he was speaking to K'ural, for though her body was awake, Shelby herself slept soundly. That had been a fascinating conversation.

As the One That Is, Shelby needed rest. She needed sleep, like any normal human being. But the Ones Who Were had no need of rest or sleep. It was strange, talking to Shelby—but not Shelby, in a way—knowing that she was asleep, even while her eyes gazed at him. As Fannon understood it, her body still needed to rest, but she could get by on a fraction of the time it took a normal human body to recuperate from a day's activities. The Ones Who Were were ever watchful. Shelby would never be vulnerable in her sleep. And when she awoke, or when the essence of her *self* awoke, she would recall everything that had been said or done, even though her self had not been aware of those things at the time. It was a remarkable phenomenon, one so obviously necessary to beings who lived in such a harsh environment, where predators could attack at any time.

Fannon was able to address Shelby, knowing that the Ones Who Were would be privy to their words, and he was also able to address the Ones Who Were specifically, knowing that Shelby would be listening and could take part in the discussion in either an active or a passive mode.

Given the intimacy of their contact, just as R'yal had learned the language by inheriting the Ones Who Were who had been with Shelby, the Ones Who Were could now converse with Fannon, using their knowledge of the language and Shelby's vocal apparatus. These discussions were necessary, but it took Fannon some time to get used to the fact that at no time was he actually speaking with an individual, in more ways than one. He could ask to speak with the Great Father, K'itar, and K'itar would respond, with Shelby being there, but only her physical self doing the talking. Nor, in speaking with K'itar, would he be speaking to an individual, but to the gestalt that was the Great Father, that infinite agglomeration of Shade males through the eons who had become "absorbed," for lack of a better concept, into the entity that was K'itar, being identified as such due to the strength and will and wisdom of that particular male ancestor, though not necessarily giving up their souls to him. In a like manner, the merging within the merging, that of the Ones Who Were within R'yal and the Ones Who Were with Shelby, had taken place with a curious result that Fannon could only begin to understand. The ancestral entities had coalesced, with K'itar, K'ural and T'lan retaining their "positions" of preeminence as Great Father, Great Hunter and Father Who Walked in Shadow respectively, while those who had been with R'yal, namely N'lia, S'eri and R'yal himself, "ascended" into the positions of Great Mother, Healer and maverick Shade.

It was R'yal who fascinated Fannon more than any of the others. R'yal had been the first Shade Fannon had ever really been exposed to, and the first Shade who had communicated directly with the humans. Also, he had been the first Shade who had ever engaged in sexual activity with a human. It was with no small degree of unease that Fannon wondered if he would be the last to do so. He could still vividly recall the shocked outrage with which he had seen that incredible tableau. It was interesting to speculate upon the fact that the body to which R'yal had responded sexually was now the body in which he found himself, literally sharing consciousness with the former object of his desire. Fannon was tempted to ask Shelby about it, but he couldn't quite bring himself to do so. Somehow it seemed like a gross violation of privacy to even ask her about her experience during the time of Need. What concerned him more, though, was how R'yal felt about being within the body of his murderer. Knowing that the memory was painful for Shelby, however, Fannon resisted following that line of inquiry. Instead, he questioned R'yal, and in so doing, the others as well, including Shelby, about his separate status, which seemed so unusual.

"But I am not separate," R'yal had said, through Shelby's lips.

"Why not?" asked Fannon, consciously reminding himself that even though he was talking to Shelby, he was directly addressing an alien being and it was that being who was responding.

"I am one of the Ones Who Were," replied R'yal. Fannon noted with some disquiet the puzzled expression on Shelby's face. The synthesis was more complete than he had imagined. The Shade was puzzled and Shelby's face mirrored his confusion. Fannon wasn't sure if it was a conscious manipulation of the Shade, if manipulation could be the proper description of R'yal's conveying facial expression, or if it was an involuntary or unconscious sympathetic reaction of Shelby's.

"True," said Fannon, "but you are not . . . uh, *with* the Great Father, or the Great Hunter."

"I am with them. They are part of me, as the Ones Who Were are part of Shelby, who is part of us."

"You don't understand," said Fannon. "K'itar is the Great Father. K'ural is the Great Hunter. What are you supposed to be, the Great R'yal?"

He fought the impulse to chuckle. It sounded like a name an entertainer might choose.

Shelby, however, chuckled. And while she chuckled, she frowned at the same time. A little bit him, a little bit her, Fannon decided. Synthesis not yet totally complete.

"R'yal is one of the Ones Who Were. R'yal was the One That Is. R'yal is R'yal. R'yal is not a Great Father. R'yal is not a Great Hunter. R'yal is not a Healer. R'yal is R'yal."

It was more difficult speaking with R'yal than with any of the others. It was becoming progressively more difficult to draw him forth.

"It's like a part of my identity resisting the rest of me," Shelby told him later. "R'yal is the greatest element of disharmony within me."

"Why don't the Ones Who Were, I mean, the others, I don't know, what do you say, take charge of him? Whip him into shape, tell him to get in line, whatever."

"You mean why don't I exert more control over R'yal?"

"Is that what I mean?"

"We are one, the Ones Who Were and I," she replied. "Becoming more unified all the time. So it's really the same thing, I suppose. Listen, Drew, I'm grateful for your interest, I really am. I *need* spending this time with you. It gives me a feeling of not having to go through it all alone. God knows, it isn't easy."

"What's the problem with . . . your R'yal aspect?" Fannon made a sour face. "Jesus, this shit is hard to talk about."

"Try living it. I guess I'm the problem," she said. She sighed and massaged the bridge of her nose. "I did kill him, after all. I just can't shake the responsibility for that. It isn't something that just goes away."

"You mean you feel guilty, so you're spoiling him by letting him have his way?"

She looked at him intensely.

"That's an incredible way of putting it," she said.

"Hell, what do I know? I'm reaching, same as you are. Was I close?"

"That part of me does seem childish," she said. "So incredibly obstinate, rebellious and resentful."

"How does it *feel*, Shelby? What's it like when you're alone? How do you interact with R'yal? Or don't you?"

"I don't," she said. She shook her head. "Drew, I never really gave it all that much thought before, believe it or not. I think we're very close to something here."

"I don't get it," he said, leaning forward, close to her. "How could you not think about it?"

"I'm getting a headache. . . ."

"Fuck your headache. We *have* to get this straight. You're not going to be one hundred percent until this synthesis thing is complete. It had better be complete by the time we get to Boomerang. How could you not think about R'yal? How can you ignore a part of yourself?"

"I—I just resist it, that's all. I can't really explain it. When I feel him strongly within me, I try to put it . . . put him out of my mind. I just . . . I guess the others make it easier, I feel stronger because of them. It's like, you know, when you get an impulse or a feeling and you try to put it out of your mind, to fight it?"

"How do you think R'yal feels about it?"

"I don't know. I won't let him get that close to me."

"He's closer to you than anyone is ever likely to get," said Fannon. Suddenly he had an insight into the situation that, if he gave voice to it, would hurt Shelby. He decided to risk it. "You *killed* him to let him get close to you, didn't you?"

She stiffened.

"Think back, Shelby," Fannon pressed on, "how did you feel when you stuck that spear in him? *What* did you feel?"

"Drew, please—"

"Come on, dammit, answer me! *Deal* with it!"

"I hated him," she said softly.

"Don't tell me, tell him."

"But he *is* me!"

"Is he? Then tell yourself. *Admit* it to yourself." He thought he understood it all suddenly. It seemed to come to him with an astonishing clarity, and he couldn't believe that he was wrong. It just . . . *made sense.*

"Shelby, you once told me, not too long ago, about how you made up your mind many years ago, before you joined the service, that no one was ever going to take from you again. That everyone you ever allowed to get close to you just took and gave nothing in return. You ran away from it then and you're running away from it now, can't you see that? You told me that *they* took them away from you, the Ones Who Were. The Ones Who Were took from you, but they also gave you a great deal, didn't they? That's why you wanted them back so much, that's why you needed them so badly that you were willing to kill for them, even though you weren't entirely yourself. Forget that, it's not important."

"Not important? If I had been whole, I never would have killed R'yal!"

"That makes a hell of a convenient excuse, but you don't know that for sure, do you?"

"God, Drew, how can you say that?"

"Because it's *true.* You don't know. *I* don't know. If someone took something from me that was as valuable, as essential to my life, as the Ones Who Were seemed to be to yours, I don't know, Shelby, I might well have killed to get it back myself. All of us can kill. Hell, you *know* that! You've got hunters within you now! You know that wounded animals kill as a reflex, as an instinct of self-preservation! R'yal wounded you when he took the Ones Who Were away. And he took more than that, he took a part of *you,* a part of your *self.* You're not guilty of anything except taking back what was yours in the only way that you knew how. *Was* there any other way?"

"No. No, there wasn't."

"R'yal followed us back from the place of mating. We didn't drag him with us, he followed on his own. The other Shades wouldn't accept him. He came back with us because he had to. The will of the All Father, remember?"

She nodded.

"Everything that happened, Shelby," Fannon said quietly, intensely, "happened because it *had* to happen."

It was one of those moments when things magically

seem to come together on their own. One of those moments when, in saying something to someone else, you realize that it applies to you, as well.

"I guess even my being here had to happen," Fannon said slowly.

It was an incontrovertible truth. He had asked for it to happen. Had asked for it by accepting the mission to Boomerang, by not leaving the service following the Rhiannon mission, when he had sworn that he would leave and never fly another mission for ColCom again. He had asked for it by postponing his retirement again and again until he was unable to retire due to circumstances beyond his control. But then, they never were beyond his control.

He had controlled everything in his life by the choices he had made. By the choice that he had made with Nils to revive their pilot when Wendy was struck down, by the choices they had made not to abort the mission when, several times, they could have. By the choice that he had made to enter the service and by his choice of ColCom as his assignment, against all the wishes of his parents.

A long, long time ago, a small boy had told his mother that he would trade people for space any old day. Even then, the choice was made.

Anderson, goddam his soul to hell, was right, Fannon realized. I left it all behind. No one twisted my arm. I damn well asked for it, every bit of it. I wanted to go to space, and leaving behind the people that I loved was the price I paid to do it. I'm sitting here like some amateur shrink trying to convince Shelby that she shouldn't feel guilty for killing the Shade when I can't get over my own guilt for killing off my past.

In a dream, he walked through a shattered, derelict ship. It was a dream he knew too well. A dream he dreaded, and yet it was a dream that he had fashioned, a dream that his subconscious mind had chosen. The ship was empty because his mother had warned him that it was lonely out in space. He kept walking through the ruined ship, a broken, ugly vessel, huge gaping holes in its hull, like the holes that had been punched through his youthful dreams. He knew what he would find when he came to that row of cryogens. He would find the price that he had paid to make his choice, the price he had never acknowledged to himself.

How much easier it was to vent his anger upon the agency he served! Colonization Command. Button-pushing opportunists, manipulators who had as little regard for the people under their command as they had for the worlds which they exploited. He resented them, and yet he served them, had continued to serve them even after the Rhiannon mission, when his sense of moral outrage had been such that he had told himself that he was willing to give up the work he loved in order not to further such mercenary, heartless interests.

Only he had stayed.

He had stayed and he had rationalized his decision by taking upon himself the role of spacer with a conscience. The noble, self-sufficient young explorer who understood that the rules existed only for the purpose of there being rules, that spacers were on their own out in the field, free to improvise and make or break the rules as they saw fit, thereby creating an artificial independence from their superiors at ColCom HQ.

"Someone has to play God," he had told Nils, after telling him the story of the Rhiannon mission.

That someone always kept on changing somehow. If it wasn't Fannon playing God by making the decision to revive Shelby from her dreams in coldsleep, thereby taking away from her forever the security of her isolation, then it was men like Anderson who played God, deciding what it was the human race was fit or not fit to know, and sending men and women, Shelby, Thorsen, and himself, on a mission to Boomerang from which they would not be allowed to return.

Very convenient, to attribute it all to "the will of the All Father." How easily he had picked up that turn of phrase! Nor was he alone. Those back on Earth who, in their lust for longer life, had decided to risk a drug that was not proved laid the blame for the result with God. Just as he laid the blame for being exiled to Boomerang on Anderson and the other men of the Directorate of ColCom. Among the many differences that separated human beings and Shades, one stood out now as being, perhaps, by far the most significant.The Shades, unlike the humans, did not confuse their own will with the will of some omniscient deity. If they perceived something as being a result of "the will of the All Father," they didn't cry about it.

Fannon abruptly became aware that he had been lost in reverie—lost within himself—for quite some time. He felt Shelby's hands in his, and he could not recall whether he had taken her hands or she had taken his. It was as though he had actually been away and time had passed with nothing changing in the interim except the passage of that time.

"Hi," said Shelby. "Welcome back."

He grinned, self-consciously.

"You know, that was a hell of a dressing-down you gave me. I suspect you're something of a Great Father yourself. I didn't know you had it in you."

"That makes two of us," he said. "You have that effect on people. The mouth just runs blithely along and suddenly the brain realizes what the mouth is saying and everything stops short. It's amazing sometimes the things you find out about yourself if you only listen to what you're saying."

She smiled. "Something very interesting just happened."

"Yeah, I'll say."

"I'm glad you're here, Drew. I think everything is going to be all right now."

Later on, Fannon couldn't recall who had made the first move. Perhaps they had both moved toward each other simultaneously. It had been nothing that was planned or even anticipated, though perhaps he had admitted the possibility to himself at some time or another. Maybe she had too. Either way, it didn't matter. It simply happened.

He felt her lips on his, and he put his arms around her, very tenderly, very gently, as though his grip could crush her. Her fingers spread out in his hair, her tongue touched his and danced around it, and they both sank down at the same time, to make soft, pleasant and unhurried love. They fell asleep next to each other, and he remembered wondering, just before sleep took him, what the Ones Who Were thought of it all. But he didn't dwell on it. Shelby was what Shelby was, and loving her meant loving them.

Somehow, at that moment, that seemed very natural. He fell asleep.

And, for once, the nightmare didn't come. It never came again.

CHAPTER TWELVE

The bridge of the *Wanderer* had the largest observation port Fannon had ever seen. It was like some huge, panoramic screen, dwarfing him. Unfortunately, the view it afforded was singularly unimpressive.

For the past several ship's days, the *Wanderer* had been accelerating steadily, the powerful Hawking drive taking them closer and closer to the speed of light. Fannon had never *seen* spaceflight. His view of space had always been limited to whatever he could see from a mission base or a shuttle or a ship's lighter; a view through the observation port of an orbital station could technically be considered a "view of spaceflight," but to Fannon it had never counted. It wasn't what he had fantasized seeing as a boy; it wasn't what the movies showed him. Reality somehow never quite lived up to what was expected of it. As the *Wanderer* hurtled through space at speeds that were impossible when Fannon had originally flown to Boomerang, the view was depressingly monochromatic.

Ahead of them was a flat, obsidian void that seemed to send off streamers of white, pale arcs that seemed to rocket past them like flashes of improbably straight lightning. The sensation was similar to that of falling into a bottomless pit, the walls of which were illuminated with sporadically placed fixtures, the speed of the fall so great that the fixtures themselves were indistinguishable, visible only by the light which they emitted, a light perceived as a colorless fiber of energy. It was, of course, no surprise to Fannon. Traveling at such a speed could not possibly afford them a view that would conform to his childish dreams of multicolored worlds and shooting stars, but still, it was a disappointment. It was a sight that he had never seen and he was quickly tired of it. Besides, staring at the view, if it could be called that, was remarkably conducive to a migraine headache. Thorsen had opened the port only briefly, for their benefit. Now, as the shutter slid across it, he turned to them and smiled.

"I told you not to expect much," he said. "It gets boring pretty quickly, doesn't it?"

Fannon shrugged.

"There's one thing that puzzles me a bit," said Shelby. She now used the words "me" and "I" purely for semantic convenience. The synthesis was now complete; what had been interrupted back on Boomerang now passed its final cycle. The stage she was at now could only be considered a form of evolution in which the concept of an ego and an id no longer applied. She was now in every sense a hybrid, not Shade, not human, something wholly different and unique.

"I haven't seen any evidence of course corrections being made," she said. "I assume that we're on course to Boomerang, but at the speed at which we're traveling, surely that necessitates almost constant adjustment, and frankly I don't even begin to see how it would be possible for anyone to—"

"Before you get hopelessly bogged down," said Thorsen, "let me anticipate the rest of your question. Yes, you're right in that it wouldn't be possible for a human to make any sort of course corrections that would make any difference at our present rate of speed, which will continue to increase until we reach almost the speed of light, or close enough to it that it doesn't really pay to worry about the difference. However, you are not taking into consideration several factors with which you're unfamiliar.

"For one thing, we're working with a guidance system that's incredibly complex and generations removed from the primitive systems you're accustomed to. While en route, the pilot really has nothing to do except worry a whole hell of a lot, because if any mistakes were made, they were made before we left and it's too late to worry about them now. Fortunately, I'm not the worrying kind. Never been terribly prone to anxiety. If you go, you go, what the hell, at least your death will be dramatic.

"Added to that is a false assumption on your part, that we are going to Boomerang. Well, we are going there, eventually, but not right away. You might say that we're heading for our departure point, past which you are going to have the pleasure of taking us in at FTL." He grinned.

Fannon glanced sharply at Thorsen and saw that, although the man was grinning, he appeared to be serious.

"I don't understand," she said. "I don't even understand how the Hawking drive is going to accomplish FTL. It doesn't make any sense. I can see how we're capable of approaching the speed of light, but—"

"That's because the Hawking drive *itself* is only a means to an end," Thorsen said. He winked at Fannon. "You're going to love this." He turned back to Shelby. "You see, what the Hawking drive will do is get us to our departure point at as near to the speed of light as it is possible to get. Now you're going to ask me what I mean by our departure point. I'll tell you."

He walked over to a computer screen and punched out a code. An animated display appeared.

"Okay, now here is where it gets really interesting. Technically speaking, FTL is not achieved by *us*—that is, the ship. Rather, it is achieved *for* us. What makes FTL possible is the technology that has enabled us to manipulate quantum black holes."

"What?"

Thorsen grinned at Fannon. "I told you you were going to love this. Pay attention, it gets better. It takes approximately four to six quantum black holes, properly manipulated, to achieve a Twilight Zone. Essentially what happens is that there are giant planetoids or asteroids upon which have been constructed *huge* Hansen magnets."

He glanced at Fannon.

"Remember I told you that there are all sorts of hardship posts now? That's an example of a real killer. The planetoids are maneuvered into position by the small crews that are based there. A real fun job. They're in charge of programming the systems governing the Hansen magnets. In effect, they pass the black hole through the magnetic field, which enables them to manipulate it. It takes several such magnet bases working in concert to create a formation of quantum black holes that will be conducive to a Twilight Zone. At the center of this formation, where gravity is canceled out, each quantum hole working against the others, we get an area of calm that should be large enough to enable a ship to pass through without all sorts of fascinating things happening to it that I'd rather not even think about, thank you. If the masses are large enough, the Schwarzchild radii of the holes should intersect, and since we would be affected by all of them equally and not be pulled into any one hole, they should cancel out as well. To put it simply, think of an iron fragment, a ball perhaps, surrounded by four magnets. Each magnet exerts its force, but if they are properly spaced, their force in concert cancels out any force at all, so the iron ball wouldn't move at all. However, within the Schwarzchild radii, physical law breaks down. And that creates the Twilight Zone, that point where the radii intersect. What we've got to do is thread that needle and we'll be at our departure point.

"Before we get there, however, all of us will enter coldsleep. This will be a somewhat different form of coldsleep than you are accustomed to, however. You will not dream. Once you are within the cryogen, you will be conditioned to enter a neutral alpha state, literally a thought-free state, a sort of free-floating nothingness. This will be to prevent any of us from interfering with the homeopathic transfer effect. Because, you see, one of us will *not* enter coldsleep. One and only one. *You*," he said to Shelby.

"The only limitation of FTL is that we can't just go anywhere at all. We must have someone on board who has been to our destination before. Preferably someone with good powers of concentration. While the rest of us are off in limbo, you"—he pointed at Shelby—"will be wide awake. And *concentrating*. You're going to have to focus all your energies, your entire *being*, on Boomerang. You have a firmer sense of belonging there than anyone else on board, much more so than our friend Fannon here. For you, Boomerang is home. Think about home, Shelby. That's all you have to do and the Twilight Zone will pop us out nicely in convenient proximity. Chances are excellent that it will spit us out right into a parking orbit."

Fannon suddenly realized that his mouth was open. He shut it with something of an effort.

"Suppose I don't think about Boomerang?" she said. "Suppose my concentration slips or something?"

"Oh, you don't want to do that," Thorsen said casually.

"*Wait* a minute," Fannon said. "You mean to tell me that *if* these Hansen magnets get lined up properly and *if* the formation of the quantum black holes is dead-on perfect so that they cancel out each other's gravitational pull and *if* these Schwarzchild radii intersect at just the right point and *if* we manage to hit that point *just* right, and *if* Shelby thinks happy thoughts . . . poof, clap your hands if you believe in fairies, and we're there?"

Thorsen pursed his lips. "Well," he said and shrugged, "I didn't say that there wasn't a certain element of risk involved."

"What happens if something goes wrong?" Fannon asked. "Suppose the radii don't intersect just right or . . . or we don't go through at the right point? What happens then?"

"Your guess is as good as mine. I've never had the opportunity to find out. Several ships were lost that way—at least I *assume* they were lost. Who's to say what is possible in a region where physical laws cease to apply? Reality becomes very surreal in the Twilight Zone. If we blow it, only Shelby's going to be around to know what happened. I think. I'm not entirely sure. Either way, it should be an interesting experience."

Fannon exhaled heavily. "To say the least."

Thorsen looked at him with amusement. "Don't tell me that the prospect bothers you?"

"No, why should it bother me? I've always wanted to dive into a black hole."

It was time.

The *Wanderer* was rushing through the cosmos at a fraction less than the speed of light. Those members of the crew who had been awake were now tucked away inside their cryogens, their thought patterns arrested, their mental states frozen in a nebulous null void. Only Thorsen, Shelby and Fannon were awake upon the bridge.

"Are you frightened?" Thorsen asked her.

"No."

"I wish there was some way I could prepare you for what you're about to experience," he said, "but I can't. I don't know what's going to happen. You have to make up your own reality within the Zone. I went through it several times myself, and it's no help. It's different for everyone. There is no stability of any kind within the Zone. Anything goes. Where the radii intersect, you're going to be the only thing that's real. For that period of time, however long it lasts, the only universe that will exist is you. There will be no gravity, there will be no ship, there will be no time. Just you. You'll be able to take us anywhere you want to go, to any place, to any time. It's one hell of a king-size responsibility. We could arrive thousands of years past the time when you left Boomerang, or we could arrive before you left. Theoretically, it's possible. In an area where time and space mean nothing, there is no reason to assume that you couldn't bring us back to Boomerang during the time that you were there. I've never heard of anything like that happening, but that doesn't mean it *couldn't* happen. It might be awkward to run into Nils, Fannon and Shelby when we get there. That might be an interesting experiment to try some time, but let's pass on it for now, okay?"

Fannon groaned. "Look, can't we just forget the whole thing? I'll tell you what, let *me* stay awake and we'll all go back to Colorado and have us a nice dinner."

Thorsen ignored him. "Just fix Boomerang firmly in your mind. Think of a time and place, I'd suggest, to make things easier on a whole lot of people, to take us back to Boomerang just after you left. That way, when I go back, I can bring the ship back a day or so after it departed from Gamma 127 and the Directorate will still be alive. Then I can make it back here, back to Boomerang, I mean, having already been there, some time after we arrive there. . . . Can you follow that?"

"I think so."

"Any questions?"

She shook her head.

"Good, because beyond what I've already told you, I haven't any answers. I'm going to leave the observation port shuttered. You really don't want to see what we're going into. It'll happen too fast for you to see anything anyway, and you'll just be thrown off."

"How will I know when we're in the area where the radii intersect?" she asked.

"You'll know. Just make yourself comfortable and start getting your mindset locked in. You're a pilot, remember. You can do it. Come on, Fannon, let's move it."

"Suppose she can't handle it?" Fannon said, when they were out of earshot, on the other side of *two* hatches; he wasn't taking any chances that she could overhear them. "Suppose she can't take the pressure?"

"Suppose anything you like," said Thorsen.

"What does that mean?"

"It means, my friend, that it makes no difference. You chose a way of life that most people only dream about. You made the choice, now take the consequences. Pay your dues. Relax, Fannon. You're going to be a time traveler. Think of the stories you'll be able to tell your grandchildren."

They came to their cryogens.

"In you go," said Thorsen. "Nothing to worry about, it's all automatic. Just lie back and put your brain on hold."

Fannon was about to reply, but the dome lid of the cryogen cut him off as it slid into place. As the blue mist began to fill the chamber, he saw Thorsen give him a quick thumbs up, and then he became dimly aware of several objects coming into contact with his head in different areas—

It was a different, vastly superior ship. She was traveling at a rate of speed she had never even dreamed of in her days as a pilot, and what lay ahead of her was unknowable. Yet one thing remained constant. Once again, there was a sleeping, this time dreamless, crew, and only the pilot was awake to see them to their destination. Only this time she was not alone. She would never be alone again.

She was more than just the One That Is now, she was the Ones That Are. Truly multifaceted, she had transcended both Shade and human forms of existence to achieve a higher plane, a multidimensional level of awareness, a union with the past and with the present and an acceptance of the future which, with all the myriad possibilities involved, she could face not as an individual, but as a new race of beings contained within one shell.

She could call upon the various levels of her self—the selves that she now was—to achieve a partial semifragmentation of persona, to bring forth consciously an aspect of her selves that was capable of independent thought and action, yet that remained an ingrained part of what the being called Shelby Michaels had become. If need be, K'ural could become manifest to guide the employment of the hunter's skill and instincts. K'itar could be brought forth to add the wisdom of the generations that "he" had become. N'lia, the strong maternal aspect, S'eri the Healer, T'lan . . . all possessing vibrant life, all inextricably part of her, all sharing in the traits and instincts and vitality of both Shade and Shelby and the blending of the two.

In an action born of desperation, in one final physical act of love meant to save a thousand thousand beings from extinction, one Shade had reached out to one woman. A being that was individual in only the physical sense, a being completely unfamiliar with the human concept of encapsulation within identity, of the security within the womb that was the Ego, this being had reached out to merge with one who knew only isolation, who knew only shields and walls and flight from others of her kind. It was a jarring impact, in the most intimate terms imaginable, of one race upon another. It could possibly be called a psychic rape, an invasion into the innermost recesses of another being's soul, except the act was done with no intent to gain control, with no intent to take or use. The invasion, for such it was, unexpected and unasked-for, was also a gift. The Shade had given her the most precious thing a Shade could give—the essence of its lives. What was born of that unprecedented, unimagined union was a being that was both human and inhuman, both male and female, both individual and legion. A being who experienced the fusion and then knew the loss, a loss so great that it was necessary to kill to regain what had been taken, for without that gift it was not possible to survive.

There was now no questioning, no agonizing over what

she had become or had once been. Shelby was. And in that knowledge, in the security of not questioning one's own existence, in knowing that the selves could support the self in any situation, in that sense of being, there was peace.

Shelby was not afraid. As the *Wanderer* stabbed into the void where the universe did not intrude, there was a momentary sensation of indescribable inertia, an agony of transition as though the known universe surrendered her into the cessation of all things with a regretful sigh of resignation. The ship ceased to exist, the hull melted away into a vapor, and only sense of self was real.

For a moment, it seemed as though Shelby would fragment into a million particles, dissolving into the elements from which she came, breaking apart like some fragile crystalline formation, shattering into an explosion of an infinity of sparkling atoms. And then they were around her, real, corporeal, surrounding her, protecting and supporting.

K'itar, lying down upon the ground, so old and feeble that he could barely move. He had sent out the Call and he was waiting. It was answered by a female, young and strong and beautiful. She reached out to him and K'itar merged into N'lia, into all the females that she was and would become.

She saw K'ural, sitting on the bank of a river she remembered, carving a piece of wood into a weapon that would hurl fist-sized seed pods with devastating accuracy. She felt his hands upon the wood, felt the satisfaction there, enjoyed the smooth hardness of the seasoned surface.

She was with S'eri the Healer as he knelt beside a bird that had fallen from its nest in its first abortive attempt at flight. She gazed intently at the creature, quieting its terror, soothing it into a state that would permit her to examine its wing to see if it was broken.

She stood side by side with T'lan, cowering in his presence as he locked eyes with the hellhound that stood between him and his weapons. The beast snarled at T'lan, padded slowly toward him, a rumbling in its throat. T'lan did not move. Not once did those feral eyes leave those of the beast. The hellhound did not move. Slowly, T'lan sank down to all fours, until his eyes were level with the beast's. They remained thus for a long moment, each taking the measure of the other, until finally it was the hound that backed away.

They all watched as a human female pushed her way through a tangled thicket to kneel down beside the torn and ruined body of a dying Shade. The Shade had been literally ripped open, and its entrails were hanging out. It was still alive, but dying fast. And there was absolutely nothing she could do to help. It would be a matter of seconds. She knelt down by the gray-skinned being and gently caressed its mane. It looked up at her, and there was no expression of pain upon its face, but there was agony in those bright violet eyes that seemed to shimmer. Even as she watched, they began to glaze. Then, for just a moment, they cleared. Slowly, the Shade reached out with one hand and touched her breast. . . .

Reality folded in upon itself and was swept away. She had a brief vision of a little girl sitting with her back against a wall, her fist shoved up against her mouth, her eyes staring at the body of her father, who had fallen to the floor, the victim of a stroke. A tall and stately man with skin the hue of steel walked up to her and took her hand, leading her away into the vastness of the void. They walked through emptiness until the man collapsed in upon himself, dissolving into silver globes that bounced across the velvet black like gobs of mercury. They reformed into trees and mountains, streams and rushing rivers, giant birds and insects that took off into the night. A tumbling crescent moon rolled across the sky, sailing out and away from her in an arc that bent back upon itself, and then the luminescent boomerang came back and passed over her head, lighting up for one brief moment the bottomless abyss beneath the bridge of stone on which she stood fighting the howling winds.

In the flickering light of a campfire, she sat staring at her feet, at the wounds made by the rocks. There was no pain, only a sense of numbness that permeated her, a detached feeling, a strange sensation of being somehow incomplete. It was a feeling of hurt, of having been abandoned. In a fugue state, she walked through the forest, aware of the crunching of dead leaves beneath her feet, aware of all the smells and sounds around her, but indifferent to them all. They seemed to belong to her no longer.

In another body, following in her own footsteps on the trail of her self, she pressed on through the forest, terrified of the frightened thing within her that had been torn away from steadying emotions by a force exerted by the Ones Who Did Not Understand. Like a fish flopping weakly on a riverbank, thrashing in the oppressive air as it sought to regain its own element, this human aspect in the body of a Shade cried out to be restored to its rightful place, to be joined with itself, to be complete once more. And, on some deep instinctual level, that part of her despaired, resigned to being forever sundered from the whole.

Blue mist settled on the forest and obliterated it. It seeped through the treetops like a substantial fog, clinging to the moss. The night grew cold and she began to dream.

Deep in the recesses of her nightmare, she awoke to stare, as if from the bottom of a pellucid pool, at a face that floated over her, a face that seemed devoid of all expression and emotion, a face that was her own. And as the part of her within the alien body sought to scream at being murdered by its self, the point of the javelin came down and a haze of stark incarnadine oblivion descended, through which a hand stretched forth in desperation. . . .

She thought of Boomerang. She thought of home. She thought of a beginning of a new existence and the trials that lay ahead. She fixed in her mind a vivid picture of the planet as she had last seen it, before their ship departed never, she had thought, to return again. The void seemed to buckle and to spasm. She was subjected to a vertiginous sensation as the blackness sucked her through, threatening to dispel the vision that she clung to. Then there was a roaring in her ears, a shaking all around her, as the place where nothing could exist rejected her reality and, without warning, the hull of the ship reappeared around her. A quick glance at the instruments showed that they were registering nothing, and then the ship was spinning into space, tumbling, it seemed, end over end as she tried to will it onto a steady course. Dimly, as though from very far away, she heard the sounds of chimes and the retracting dome lids of the cryogens. She heard running footsteps coming closer, hatches opening and shutting, and then she looked up at the observation port, open now, displaying a view of a world the color of an emerald. And, for just the briefest moment, she thought she saw the glint of sun off the hull of another ship as it left the orbit of the planet to begin its journey home.

"Nice going, Shelby," she heard Thorsen's voice behind her. "You got us there. I never doubted that you could."

And she heard Fannon's slow expulsion of pent-up breath and smiled. She leaned her head back against the soft cushioning material of the pilot's chair and turned around to see them.

Their eyes grew wide. Thorsen simply stared at her in amazement. Fannon swallowed hard and muttered, "Jesus Christ."

Her hair had turned snow white and her eyes shimmered with a startling violet glow.

EPILOGUE

Fannon put down his fork and sipped from the glass of wine before him. "Not bad," he said, "but you know, somehow the meat of these monsters always tasted better when cooked over an open fire." He chuckled. "What do you say we have a barbecue some night, for old times' sake?"

Shelby smiled. "Why not? But you'd better make it a night when I'm not too hungry. I might get impatient and start eating raw meat. And judging from your reaction the first time you saw me do it, I'd say that might ruin your evening." Her violet eyes held a faint light of mockery.

Fannon grimaced with distaste. "Yeah, that did get to me, all right. Intellectually, I was aware that Shades don't cook their food, but the sight of you wolfing down raw flesh was enough to damn near put me in shock."

It had happened on one of their first nights following their return to Boomerang. They had been hiking through the wild in search of Shades. Shelby had not yet had an opportunity to fashion a new catapult for herself, but she had made a javelin, which she carried. There was no real need for it, since she could use her modern weapon—her human weapon—to defend herself, but the javelin seemed more intrinsic to her environment and sense of selves than the rifle. She had worn the rifle slung across her shoulder; the javelin she carried loosely in her right hand. Without warning, she had suddenly let fly with the spear at what, to Fannon, seemed like nothing more than an innocent clump of bushes. Yet as the spear struck home, he could hear the howl of the hellhound, and he had not even had the time to bring his own weapon to bear before Shelby raced forth to finish the animal off. Fannon had never even seen it, even with his hunter's eyes. Later, after they had skinned and dressed the beast, and Fannon was anticipating a tasty supper cooked over an open fire, he had stared aghast as Shelby took a piece of the red meat, tearing into it with ravenous appetite. It had made him feel dizzy with nausea.

He smiled at the memory of the sight, in spite of himself. "Yeah, that took my breath away, all right. You still take a whole lot of getting used to. You know what had me scared worse than anything else? I was terrified of what would happen when the Shades went into their rutting stage, that time of Need."

"Why didn't you tell me?" she said.

"Sure! How was I supposed to do that? I can see myself bringing up the damn subject. 'Listen, Shelby, about this time of Need thing . . .' No way. I could just see myself waking up one morning to find you gone, off to that goddam mountain once again."

"I know," she said. "But it's a trip we're going to have to make, sooner or later."

"You mean when the time comes around again you're actually going to go? Christ, do you *have* to?"

She had to laugh at the pained expression on his face. "No, that isn't what I meant. I meant that we should make the trip only because it's the only time Shades ever group together. We have to do it, if only in the interests of science. I admit that maintaining a sense of scientific detachment is going to take a considerable effort of will on my part, but I think I'll manage. One of the curious side effects of the merging is the discovery by my Shade aspects of the fact that humans are in Need virtually all the time. Whenever I start getting turned on by you, I have to fight the urge to stop and passively observe the phenomenon of my feelings. It's something new to me, and I don't mean only because I'm part Shade." She grinned. "Still, don't be surprised if I rape you when the Need comes. Think your male ego can handle that?"

"I think so," he replied, "but I don't know if my heart could stand it."

"It had better or I'll find myself a younger lover. And not necessarily a human one."

"All right, rub it in. But just remember what happened last time you tried that."

"I don't think I'll ever forget," she said. "It's so strange. I think of them as being my people, just as humans are my kind, but when they see me, they're terrified."

The jocular mood of their dinner conversation had taken a serious tone. Outside their dome, it was night on Boomerang, a still, warm and lovely night, its silence only occasionally broken by the sounds of beasts of prey.

"If only I could establish some sort of contact," she said. "I've tried speaking to them, but even though I know their language, I can only pronounce a few of their words. And it's been so long since the language was actually spoken out loud by One That Is that my trying it even creates a further barrier." She sighed and leaned back in her chair, eyes closed. "If there's a way, I haven't found it yet."

"You will," said Fannon. "We've got lots of time. You know, it's really kind of funny. When we first came here, the place gave me the creeps. I couldn't stand it and I couldn't wait to get away. But it's really different now. We're not alone. We've got our own little colony right here, and knowing that this maudlin feeling that creeps up on me every now and then is just a result of the projection of the Shades makes it easier to live with. Still, I don't think I could have done it without you."

She chuckled. "You don't respect me for my body, you just want me for my minds."

"Cute. But it may be true for all I know. I don't analyze those things. Hell, I'd never figure it out anyway. One thing's for sure, though. The way you are now, you'd kill 'em back on Earth."

There was a long pause.

"I'm sorry, Drew," she said, reaching out to take his hand. "I'm truly sorry that you won't be going back there."

He shrugged. "I'm a spacer. At least, that's what I keep telling myself." His fingers toyed with his fork. "I don't think I'll ever be the spacer Thorsen is, though. I'm an atavism, just as Anderson said. I thought Thorsen had to be some sort of machine to take being sent out here so casually. After that trip here, though, I know better. To have to live with that mode of travel takes something I don't have. I could never be so nonchalant about my life. There's a different breed of spacer now. It's really quite romantic. They live for the moment. They thrive on incredible risk, and each time they come through it in one piece, it's an unexpected bonus. I would've thought that you and I fit into that category, but it just ain't so. Hell, you're in a category all by yourself, but me, no, I guess I've found where to draw my line."

"It's just a matter of degree, Drew."

"Isn't everything? No, I'm past it now. They can have their FTL—I actually prefer coldsleep. Especially now that I don't get nightmares all the time. And that one in particular seems to be gone for good. Still, I wouldn't mind taking one more FTL flight."

"Back to Earth."

"It *could* happen, Shelby. It could. It's about the only thing that keeps me going. I've worked it out. We can travel faster than light now, but time still goes by. A lot of time goes by even while a ship is accelerating to near light speed. People like Thorsen can travel back and forth through time by FTL, so long as they don't disturb the continuum; they're afraid of trying that, but even as we sit here now, the people we saw back on Gamma 127 are long dead. They must have known, when they sent us out here, that we couldn't come back to their time, because the situation really wouldn't have changed. People would still be scared of Shades, they would resent them, hate them, take it out on those who brought the information back, God only knows, but time *will* change that. Anderson was right. We can't return to the past. But we can go back to the future. It could be done!"

"How?"

"The time will come when the memory of that drug won't be so painful. Hell, they'll probably even forget. They've forgotten history throughout the ages. When that happens, they might be more receptive to finding out about a race of beings that never die. Jake Thorsen will be coming back to us. And then we'll have the ship again. All we have to do is finish our work here and he can take us back, back to the future!"

"In theory, that might work," she said. "But you're forgetting that we still have to find a way to establish a rapport with the Shades. *I* have to find a way."

"You *will!*"

"And you're also forgetting that going into the future could disturb the time continuum. They've been so careful about that. Jake's gone back to a time where he *belongs.* His arrival there will not upset things. What you're talking about has never been tried before. Jake said that ships have been lost within the Twilight Zone. Maybe they were lost because they came out in the wrong time, at a place where they belonged, but not the time. It may be possible, but it would be taking an incredible chance."

"Jake's breed take chances all the time."

"But do you have the right to ask him to take *this* one?"

He stared deep into her burning eyes. When he spoke, his voice was almost a whisper. "You don't want me to go back, do you? Because *you* don't want to go back."

"I don't know, Drew. I really, honestly don't know." She paused. "I've got a confession to make. I haven't told anyone about this. When we came out of the Twilight Zone, for a moment, just for a moment, I thought I saw a ship."

He frowned, not comprehending.

"*Our* ship, Drew. Our ship as we were leaving Boomerang. The ship with you, Wendy, Nils, R'yal and me aboard."

Understanding dawned. "My God. My God, then it *can* be done!"

"I *thought* I saw it, Drew. I can't be sure. You can't imagine what it was like, coming through. Perhaps there was nothing there at all. It seemed real, I could have sworn it was our ship, but I—*don't know.*"

"Yes, but if there's a *chance* . . ."

"It's not for me to decide," she said. "You're the one who's going to have to decide whether or not to ask Jake to take that chance. I think he'd do it. And if it worked, you'd both be heroes. Or maybe villains. I don't blame them for being scared to try it. But it's something you're going to have to decide for yourselves."

"Would you come with us?"

"I can't answer that right now. But I wouldn't stand in your way."

They had been on Boomerang almost a month when Jake Thorsen returned with the ship. And Nils. Fannon had been overjoyed to see him. He hadn't realized just how much he had missed the tall Swede. Nils had brought a bottle of champagne along to help celebrate their reunion, and he had even thought to pack several cases of cigarettes for Fannon, knowing how much his friend liked the outmoded and unhealthful vice of smoking. Nils had been shocked at Shelby's appearance, but after the initial jolt had worn off, he too had fallen prey to her magnetism. It was incredibly easy to become fixated upon her. Not only had her physical appearance become compelling and electrifying—it was almost impossible to look away from those shining violet eyes—but her self-assurance and her literal animal qualities combined to make her a truly commanding presence. She had become, within a short time, very special to everyone at Boomerang Base.

There had been much to discuss, and they found themselves tripping over each other's words, anxious to catch up, but the evening finally settled down into a pleasant mode of relaxation that only friends who are truly warm and secure in each other's presence can enjoy. It had been a difficult time for Nils, and he had gone through exhaustive therapy, but he was finally rid of the torments of space fever. Of Wendy Chan, he had no news. Her sleeping body had been returned to Earth, where it was hoped that her sleeping mind could be revived. They toasted absent friends.

The work on Boomerang Base was proceeding quickly. Already, several permanent structures had been finished, and they now had a fully operational laboratory. Contact with the Shades had still not been established, which was a source of some distress to Shelby, but the situation was one that could not and would not be forced. Shelby recalled only too well—and knew only too well—how the

Shades perceived them. Fear and ignorant prejudice were things that could be overcome only by time.

They were not ignored, however. Although the Shades shied away from direct personal contact, they knew that they were daily being observed, as R'yal had observed them once before. Every man and woman at the base had as complete an understanding of the Shades as it was possible to have without actually experiencing the phenomenon of merging. Shelby had seen to that. At times, when the psychic emanations of the Shades nearby were particularly strong, it became difficult for the humans at the base. Some were more susceptible than others, as in the case of Wendy Chan, but if the sense of isolation began to become unbearable, they sought out Shelby, in whose presence they found solace to a great degree. It was the greatest hardship of the mission, having to live with the direct sense impressions of the Shades' perceptions of them. But knowing the feelings for what they were helped a great deal, and they all found strength within each other, as well as in the knowledge that the time was bound to come when the Shades would realize that humans were not lost and lonely beings that had been cursed by the All Father. There had to be a way to let them know the truth, and in time they knew that they would find it.

One night, when they were all alone, Fannon had broached the subject of going back to a future Earth to Jake. And he had told him of what Shelby believed she had seen when they reentered the fabric of real space near Boomerang.

"I've already mentioned it to Nils," he said. "I haven't told any of the others because I wanted to know how you felt about it first. It's asking a lot, I know, but how do you feel about it?"

Jake considered it for a while in silence.

"Don't think I haven't thought about it myself once or twice," he said. "Not about going back to Earth, specifically, but I've thought about the possibility of what might happen if, for example, I was piloting an FTL flight back to a place where I had been before and something went wrong with my innate time sense. Suppose my concentration wasn't strong enough, for instance, and I wound up arriving back at Gamma 127 before all of us had left for

Boomerang. Could the same ship occupy two places in the same time? Could I meet *myself*? What would happen? It's an intriguing possibility, isn't it?"

He leaned his elbow on the table and raised his hand to rub his mouth in a thoughtful fashion.

"Hmmm. If what Shelby saw really was your ship, then it *is* possible. If that is, in fact, what she saw. The Zone can really do a number on your mind. So maybe we can go back to a part of the past that we occupied, physically speaking, at the same time as we had occupied that space. As far as anybody knows, anything is possible within the Zone. It all depends upon how careful you are about your mindset. But it's a question I haven't contemplated alone. Earth's scientists have been agonizing over it. It scares them, and I can understand that. As for the future . . . I don't know. There is no *specific* future, theoretically. There are an infinite number of potential futures. The past is specific, we *know* what happened, at least insofar as we are concerned, but the future? That's a question that's puzzled writers, scientists and philosophers for generations. If we can go into the future, does that mean that we would change the past by our presence there? Or would we go into *a* future and affect a past other than that which was the past we knew? Or would there be no effect at all?"

Fannon nodded morosely. "Yeah, I see. Well, I knew it was a lot to ask. I guess I just never really thought it through the way you have. I won't bring it up again."

"Oh, I didn't say I wouldn't do it."

"What?"

Thorsen regarded him with a steady gaze. "You don't really know yourself as well as you think you do."

"What do you mean?"

"I mean that you've primed yourself for quitting so well that you've started thinking of yourself as some sort of has-been spacer, a man past both his prime and time. We've gone too fast for you." He smiled. "With FTL, even in the most literal sense. Space travel has changed, you're thinking, and the change is such that it's left no place for you, the rustic pioneer of the sublight survey ships. The new spacers are just a bunch of fatalistic adventurers with whom you have nothing in common. We've gone beyond your level of 'acceptable risk.' And yet here you sit, actively considering a prospect that has virtually every FTL spacer scared shitless." Thorsen shook his head. "You're not ready to quit yet, Fannon. You're just barely getting started." Thorsen got a faraway look in his eyes. "God, it would really be something if we pulled it off, wouldn't it?"

"Then you'll *do* it?"

"It's still too early to think about it," Jake replied. "We have yet to make contact with the Shades. Don't forget, that's what we're here for. When that happens, we'll call a meeting of the base personnel. We'll put it to a vote. If the majority of them are willing to give it a shot, we're going to have to give anyone who doesn't want to try it the option of remaining behind. It's what they would have done anyway. But I think you might be surprised at our people. They're a game bunch."

"You don't think it would scare them?"

"Of course it would scare them. I'd be worried if it didn't. But then if you play it safe all your life, you'll probably wind up living a very long and very dull existence." He got up and prepared to depart. "Anyway, it's something to look forward to."

After Jake had left, Fannon sat by himself for a long while, thinking. For the first time in a long time, he felt genuinely excited. He took another cigarette and went out for a breath of air.

The compound was empty and the crescent moon slowly tumbled overhead. There were people still awake, judging by the lights inside the buildings, and work was still going on in the laboratory, but Fannon was alone outside. Staring out into the darkness of the forest, he thought about what Jake had told him and realized that he was right. He was still a spacer. He would always be a spacer. He had known it from that first day when, as a child of eight, he had seen his first shuttle taking off from Cheyenne Mountain. Time hadn't passed him by. He would pass by time.

As he stood there and smoked, he suddenly became aware of a feeling of melancholy coming over him. Knitting his eyebrows, he stared hard out past the Sturmann Field. There, just past the final stretch of trees, next to the trail they had cut, was a pair of softly glowing eyes. He moved toward them. As he came closer, he could see the Shade, standing there, watching him.

"Damn you," he muttered. "You'll stand there and watch all night, but you won't act. What in God's name does it take to break through to you? *What does it take?*"

In a helpless fit of frustration, he took the stub of the cigarette out from between his lips and flung it with all his might in the direction of the Shade. And, as he did so, he tripped over a newly protruding rootlet and fell sprawling. He did not hurt himself, but he remained lying on the ground, upon his stomach, hands spread out and digging at the soil, fingers scrabbling at the dirt.

"Fuck. What the hell's the use?"

He raised his head after a moment and saw a startling thing. The Shade had moved forward, closer to the edge of the Field, when it saw him fall. And now, still looking at him intently, it slowly sank to its knees and stretched out upon the ground in a position similar to his.

"What the . . . ?" And suddenly he understood. "Holy shit! What a bunch of fools we've been! It's the way they *pray*, for Christ's sake!" He leaned down and kissed the ground. "All Father, if you're there, I love you!" And then he shouted at the top of his lungs.

"Shelby! *Shelby! Shelby, come quick, for God's sake! We've done it! We've done it!*" I've done it, he thought. Like a blundering idiot, but I've done it. We've broken through to them. Okay, Jake, let's talk about that trip now.

He heard doors slamming and the sound of running footsteps.

"You were right, Jake. Ole Fannon's not ready to quit just yet. I'm just barely getting started. This is only the beginning."

AFTERWORD

A writer is a sort of funnel, a vessel through which the wine is poured. It's as though the ideas are out there somewhere in the ether and the writer is the focal point through which they flow. Writing is a craft, but there is a certain amount of metaphysics involved. And it helps to be able to look at the world with a constant sense of wonder. The *Moody Blues* said it best in song. Seeing "with the eyes of a child." It's certainly no great perception on their part; poets and philosophers have known about this for years. But parents forget. They get annoyed with a child who constantly asks "Why?" Kids can get into a whole litany of whys. Those of us who aren't slapped down for it sometimes grow up to be writers, because that's what writers do. They ask "Why?" or "What if?" However, you can't ask why or what if when your whole being is busy asking "How?" That's what happens when you finish a book. While you're writing it, the child is in the driver's seat. The moment that you finish, the pragmatic adult takes over. The adult suffers the anxieties and worries about how the problems are going to be solved. The child doesn't understand why there is a problem. In order to get back that sense of wonder that allows me to regress and get in touch with that child within me, I have to go through all that adult nonsense, such as worrying about what I'm going to do next, how I'm going to do it, where the money's going to come from, and when inspiration's going to hit. I have to go through it because while I was writing, I was going through a learning process, a growing up process that resulted in my becoming an adult again once the book was finished. Now I have to start over again and get in touch with the child, only the adult doesn't like to let go. The adult is terribly pompous and deadly serious and not too much fun to have around. The adult wants to be professional; he wants to hammer out the story, building it in a technical fashion. The child just delights in watching the story unfold all by itself. The adult takes himself far too seriously and makes life far too complicated. The child just wants to play, to be allowed to dream.

The Ones Who Were within us are the children. The child is the one who imagines being a Great Hunter, having an ability to be close to the beasts. The child invents imaginary playmates like the Shades. The child hears the voices of the Ones Who Were while the adult is too full of himself to listen. So now, on this chilly autumn evening, I sit back having finished this book and already the anxiety over what I'm going to do next is beginning to gnaw at me. Writing is a drug and the withdrawal symptoms are terrible to behold. I have no idea what I'm going to do next and the adult in me finds that frightening. Yet I know that sooner or later, the adult's foolish behavior will exhaust him and the child will surface with a mischievous grin to ask, "Have you had enough? Are you finished now? Because it's my turn."

The child will begin to dream and the adult, the One That Is, will be appropriately guided in the task. For it is the children within us who are the dreamers. The children are the Ones Who Were. And, as Shelby would tell you, the Ones Who Were are wiser than we can ever hope to be.

—Nicholas Yermakov
Merrick, New York

NICHOLAS YERMAKOV was born on September 30, 1951, in New York City. He has been a rock musician, an actor, an armed guard for a private police force in Beverly Hills, a journalist, a factory worker, a motorcycle salesman, a book store clerk, a disc jockey, a bartender, a dishwasher, and a radio production specialist for the United Nations.

A fulltime writer, his work has appeared in *Fantasy and Science Fiction*, *Heavy Metal*, *Galaxy*, and several anthologies, as well as in several nonfiction publications. He is the author of *Journey From Flesh*, as well as the forthcoming *An Affair Of Honor* and *Clique*. He currently makes his home in Merrick, Long Island.